COME AWAY WITH ME

ERIKA KELLY

Dear Melissa,
Enjoy!
Erik

PRAISE FOR THE CALAMITY FALLS
SERIES

KEEP ON LOVING YOU

"I adored this book! It is exactly what I love in a second-chance romance. The characters are so vibrant and real, I was rooting for them with every page." —*USA Today* Bestseller Devney Perry

"KEEP ON LOVING YOU is such a fun and sexy second-chance romance that I didn't want it to end. Their connection is a swoony blend of tender first love and sizzling heat, and Erika Kelly delivers a highly entertaining and sigh-worthy romance that shouldn't be missed."

—Mary Dube, USA Today

WE BELONG TOGETHER

"I loved every sweet, heart-wrenching, crazy, mixed-up minute of this book. It was an emotional journey from the first chapter to the last. This is Erika Kelly at her best, and this is a not-to-be-missed book!" —Sharon Slick Reads, Guilty Pleasures Book Reviews

"Erika Kelly damn near pulled my heart from my chest with Delilah and Will's story. It's so well-written that you feel everything. My heart got tugged so hard! I honestly cried at a few moments in the book. I fell all the way in love with "Wooby." It's hard not to, really." —Ree Cee's Books

THE VERY THOUGHT OF YOU

"Wow, THE VERY THOUGHT OF YOU was simply OUTSTANDING! This second chance, friends to lovers romance is enchanting and entertaining." —Spellbound Stories

"I just finished this story, and I want to start all over again. Or maybe at the start of series. To once again feel the events, the emotions, that brought these amazing characters together. To hear the banter and the arguments, the sorrow, the loss and the happiness that brought a family together and closer." —Nerdy, Dirty, and Flirty

JUST THE WAY YOU ARE

"An alpha cowboy and a smart, sassy princess collide in JUST THE WAY YOU ARE in Erika Kelly's latest, and it was fabulous! I was cheering for Brodie and Rosalina with every page. If you love stories with heart, steam, and plenty of swoon, don't miss this one!" —USA Today Bestselling Author J.H. Croix

"With the Calamity Falls series, Kelly doesn't shy away from charming. She captivates with delectable characters that wrap themselves around a heart. From the first hello to the final goodbye, Rosalina and Brodie are a match made out of the unpredictable, but the sweetest kind of heaven. JUST THE WAY YOU ARE is the perfect example of why I am hooked on this series. SWOONWORTHY READ!" — Hopeless Romantic Book Reviews

IT WAS ALWAYS YOU

"This book was full of every emotion you could ever feel. Gigi and Cassian proved you can conquer anything with true love." —Cat's Guilty Pleasure

"I could not put this book down! Erika Kelly always delivers a great love story and never disappoints! I recommend this book for romance lovers looking to get lost in a great love story." —Reading in Pajamas

CAN'T HELP FALLING IN LOVE

"I love everything about this emotional and sexy, second chance story. Erika Kelly writes a story that makes me feel like I'm right there with the two main characters, Beckett and Coco. It is a slow burn, passionate story with lots of underlying tension. I not only enjoyed this story, but I found it impossible to put down." —Cocktails and Books

TITLES BY ERIKA KELLY

The Calamity Falls series
KEEP ON LOVING YOU
WE BELONG TOGETHER
THE VERY THOUGHT OF YOU
JUST THE WAY YOU ARE
IT WAS ALWAYS YOU
CAN'T HELP FALLING IN LOVE
COME AWAY WITH ME
WHOLE LOTTA LOVE

Rock Star Romance series
YOU REALLY GOT ME
I WANT YOU TO WANT ME
TAKE ME HOME TONIGHT
MORE THAN A FEELING

Wild Love series
MINE FOR NOW
MINE FOR THE WEEK

Sign up for my newsletter to find when WHOLE LOTTA LOVE
goes live January 2021. And get PLANES, TRAINS, AND
HEAD OVER HEELS for FREE! I hope you'll come hang out

with me on Facebook, Twitter, Instagram, Goodreads, and Pinterest or in my private reader group.

COME AWAY WITH ME

Erika Kelly

ISBN-13: 978-0-9992585-4-5

Cover design and Formatting by Serendipity Formatting

Editing by Kristy Stalter deBoer

PROLOGUE

ONE ARM ACROSS HER WAIST, SKYLAR JAMES PACED THE length of the guest cottage. *Oh, my God.*

Where are you Eddie? She checked her phone for the millionth time in three days.

Still nothing.

Who walks away after getting news like that?

And what did it mean?

It's the middle of the semester. He can't just leave school, can he? He had to come back. *We have classes.*

She paced back to the window. *Are you serious right now? Who cares about classes?*

"Skylar?" her mom called. "Where are you? Get back here and help us string up these lights." And then to someone else, she muttered, "I don't know what's gotten into her lately."

"She's twenty," her aunt said. "Hormones."

With tears blurring her vision, Skylar quietly shut the window. She wanted to help her mom, but she couldn't. She couldn't think, couldn't eat, couldn't sleep…

And she couldn't tell anyone why. Not until she talked to Eddie and came up with a plan.

Her phone vibrated.

Eddie?

Her hopes crashed when she saw her dad's name on the screen.

Dad*: Chef showed up in ladybug crocs. You're going to pee your pants.

Another one came in. Her brother.

Griffin*: Did you take my iPad? Give it back or I'll hunt you down.

The words hit her brain like raindrops splattering on a windshield. Nothing registered, nothing got in.

She needed her boyfriend.

They'd been together five years. They loved each other. The longer he stayed away, the easier it was for him to make a decision without her. She needed to tell him they could do this.

We'll be fine.

She threw herself onto the bed, the down comforter and pillows swallowing her up.

With every second that passed, the anxiety grew bigger.

He's not abandoning me. He wouldn't do that. *God.* She yanked the pillow out from under her head and covered her face with it. She breathed in the lavender housekeeping sprayed on the linens.

A sudden wave of nausea rolled through her. She shot off

the bed and ran into the bathroom. Of course, at that exact moment, her phone pinged with another text.

Fighting back the bile, she willed herself to not throw up. *Not now.* On unsteady feet, she hurried back into the main room and picked up her phone.

The sight of his name on the screen sent a rush of relief through her.

Eddie*:* **Where are you?**
Skylar*:* **Guest room ten.**
Eddie*:* **Here.**

What does that mean? Here, as in their hometown of Calamity, Wyoming? Here, as in The Homesteader Inn, her family's lodge? But she didn't bother asking. She couldn't. Instead, she raced back into the bathroom and knelt.

Once she'd emptied her stomach, she rinsed her mouth with handfuls of cold water and then scraped her fingers through her hair. He couldn't see her looking a wreck and smelling like puke.

A rap at the door had her skipping the towel and drying her hands on her leggings instead. On her way, fear spilled into her bloodstream, swelling under her skin. When she'd first told him, he'd been so angry. He'd have calmed down by now, though. Accepted the reality of the situation. *God, I hope so.*

But what if he was breaking up with her? No, that made no sense.

You don't bail on the woman you love at a time like this.

Of course not. He'd just needed some time to figure things out.

3

This is huge. He had to wrap his head around it, and now he's back with a plan.

Well, good. She had one, too. Which meant, between them, they'd be okay.

We got this.

His shadow fell across the windowpanes on the side of the door. That rocking motion meant he was anxious, transferring his weight from one foot to the other.

She opened it, wanting more than anything to jump into his arms and wrap her legs around his hips. *Thank God you're back.*

But everything in her came to a screeching halt. Because that man on the doorstep was *not* Eddie. Her boyfriend was energetic, full of ideas. Her boyfriend loved her. Wanted her all the time.

This man was stern, angry, shut down. This man was a stranger.

"Where've you been?" She whispered it so her family, probably still stringing lights in the courtyard, wouldn't hear her.

Eddie didn't answer, just slipped in around her—arching away so he wouldn't make contact—and stood in the middle of the room. He gave a chin nod to the door, and she shut it.

"Do you still insist on having this baby?"

Insist? He sounded so cold, so…mean. "Yes…of course." *What kind of question is that?*

"And you agree I've made myself clear that I don't want it. I don't want to be a father. Right?"

He had. When she'd told him the results of the pregnancy test, he'd flipped out. Holding both sides of his head, he'd shouted at her to "just get rid of it." She'd told him she couldn't do that. This was their baby.

"Yeah? So? It's not about what we *want*. It's about what's happening. Ready or not, we're having a baby." She read his eyes, his expression, looking for the softening. Eddie often came down hard on an issue, but she'd always been able to tease and flirt and get him to come around. Because he loved her. And he liked to make her happy.

But she saw no love in him at all. Her pulse jackhammered, and her skin went clammy.

He pulled something out of his back pocket. An envelope. Handed it to her.

Fear squeezed her lungs so hard she went dizzy. Her trembling hands had a hard time unfolding the letter. The words jumped on the page. "What is this?" The language was stilted, formal. "Did you talk to a *lawyer*?"

"No, I don't need anyone to tell me I have rights. It's your body, so I can't stop you from going through with this, but you don't get to make decisions that affect my entire life."

"Okay, I don't know what you're talking about right now, but like it or not we're having a baby."

"No, *you* are." He waved at the paper. "I've signed away my rights. I don't want to be a father. I told you that, and you insist on doing it anyway. Well, that's bullshit." His voice rose. "You can make the decision for yourself, but you can't make it for me."

"Shh." Her stomach wrenched. What if her parents heard? Her dad was in the kitchen, but her mom was out there somewhere.

He drew in a breath to calm himself down. "You've

made your choice, and I've made mine." He pointed to the letter. "It's signed and notarized by Jeff."

Notarized? By his *drummer?* "Eddie, stop it. You're scared. I get that. I'm terrified. But we've got this. Our parents will be disappointed, but you know they'll help us." *Where are you, Eddie?* This cold, detached stranger was freaking her out. She stepped closer to him. "We love each other."

He backed away. "If you loved me, you'd get rid of it. Look, we had a verbal contract. After we graduated college, we were moving to Los Angeles, so I could play in clubs and get discovered and you could be a stylist to movie stars. That's what we agreed on."

"We can still do that. We can have a baby and still reach our dreams. Our families will help us while we finish college, and then when we move, we'll take turns watching the baby. You can watch her during the day, and I'll watch her at night while you're gigging."

"No." He shook his head. "That's a clear breach of our contract."

"What is the matter with you? You sound like an idiot right now. You're not a lawyer, you're my boyfriend. There's no *contract*. We're just two people who had dreams…and a lot of sex and sometimes forgot to use condoms."

"You're supposed to be on the pill."

"And yet, after finals, you surprised me with a camping trip and didn't think to pack my pills."

He got wild-eyed. "This is not my fault. And, more importantly, there's a simple solution. It's only a few weeks old. It's not a baby. It's not anything. It's just a ball of cells."

"It's *our* ball of cells, you jackass. And if you think for one second I'm going to kill a baby we made out of love, then you're not the guy I thought you were." She had to calm down. Bring Eddie back—not push him away. But she couldn't take a full breath. Her mind was fogged over, and she couldn't form a single, clear thought. "Look, this is the scariest thing in the world. I get that. But we can do this. We love each other, and we'll be good parents. We'll have both our families helping us. Listen to me, Eddie, we can do this."

He turned to stone. "I'm dropping out of college, and I'm heading to LA on Saturday. Me and Jeff are going together."

A hail of darts rained down on her, piercing her skin. If she looked down, she'd see blood trickling down her body. "You're leaving me behind?" *No. No, no, no.* She couldn't do this on her own.

"*You* did this. Not me. I told you to terminate the pregnancy. I told you what I wanted, and you ignored me. If you insist on doing this without my consent, then you're doing it alone." He started for the door.

"It doesn't work like that. You can't just walk away from me. From your baby." But he kept going, and when his hand touched the doorknob, she lost it. "You can't just leave. You have to help me. I can't do this alone." Her voice hit the walls, bounced back, and battered her.

He shook his head. "I don't have to do anything, because I relinquish all rights."

"Oh, my God, if you say that one more time, I'm going to punch you in the face."

Images shuffled through her mind like a deck of cards. Alone in a hospital bed. Holding a newborn—with no

7

idea what to do—*how do you bathe her? How do you feed her?*

Where am I going to live? She needed so many things. Crib, diapers, bottles. With each image, the panic spun faster until she thought her blood, tissues, and organs would fly right out of her body.

And then the fucker opened the door.

She charged forward, her palm slapping it shut. "Oh, no, you don't. I'm not going to raise our baby by myself. I can't pay for everything on my own."

"Then get rid of it, because I'm not paying a dime of child support for a kid I *told* you I don't want. My choice in this is just as valid as yours." He jerked the door open and stepped outside.

She followed him, no longer caring who heard. Her boyfriend of five years, the father of her baby, was actually walking out of her life. He was going to abandon her, make her go through pregnancy and parenting alone. She was going to die. "It doesn't work like that, you jerk. Your stupid piece of paper doesn't mean anything."

"It's signed and dated. I relinquish my rights."

That's it. Rage popped like a balloon and propelled her onto his back, but he whipped around so hard, she fell off.

"What the hell's going on?" Griffin, her oldest brother—all six-four inches of inked badassery—came out of cottage five, hair mussed and shirtless. A curtain hitched, and his dark-haired hookup peered out the window.

But Skylar ignored them. Sweaty, frantic, she shoved Eddie. "You don't get off scot-free. It doesn't work like that. And let me tell you something right now. You will pay me child support every month until this child turns eighteen, or

I'll send all four of my brothers, plus my cousin…his entire fucking football team…to collect it."

Fear flared in Eddie's eyes, and he cut a look to Griffin.

With a menacing demeanor, her brother stood like a warrior, clearly restraining himself. In that moment, she'd never loved him more.

"I don't have any money," Eddie said. "And I'm not going to for a long time."

Griff started for him, but Skylar held up her hand. "Then you'll get a job. Just like I'll have to do." She only had a year left of college—she didn't want to drop out.

But she'd figure that out later.

"This isn't fair." Eddie stood there for a long moment, his struggle playing across his features. All his righteous indignation turned to uncertainty, but with Griff standing there like a bull ready to charge, Eddie deflated.

He turned and left.

Skylar watched him go until the rage, fear, and disbelief bled out of her.

And then her knees gave out.

Thank God her brother was there to catch her.

1

FIVE YEARS LATER

WHERE ARE YOU, GRIFFIN?

Skylar James shifted her grumpy little boy to her other hip, as she pulled a blouse off the free-standing rack in her office. "I've got another one for you to try."

Her client's hand reached out from behind the curtain. "Oh, good. I'd like to lose some more weight before I wear this one." She exchanged the shirt she'd just tried on for the new one.

Her son shifted restlessly in her arms. He hadn't been sleeping well, and he'd refused to nap today. He was the sweetest boy in the world, and she hated to see him uncomfortable. Was he coming down with something…maybe an ear infection?

She reached for one of the toys he'd gotten for Christmas. "Do you want to play with this until Uncle Griff comes?" Her oldest brother had gotten him a train set he'd promised to set up that afternoon.

Skylar loved her family—loved how easily they'd accepted her unplanned pregnancy. But, as much love as they gave Rocco, absolutely nothing could take away from the fact that he didn't have a father.

Right now, at four, he didn't notice. Soon, though, he would.

And it broke her heart.

Her son shook his head, rubbing his eyes with the back of a chubby little hand.

"As soon as Uncle Griff gets here, he's going to take you upstairs and set up the tracks. Won't that be fun?" To save money, they lived out of her office. The downstairs salon had a dressing room and fancy full-length mirror, her desk, clothing racks, a bathroom, and a kitchen. The bedrooms were upstairs.

Again, Rocco shook his head.

Please don't have a melt-down in front of my client.

This is exactly why I don't mix work and family.

As he grew more restless, she knew she had to do something. Finding the holiday playlist on her phone, she skipped ahead to DMX's "Rudolph, the Red-Nosed Reindeer," keeping the volume low.

As soon as it came on, she bounced along to it, relieved to see her son's shy smile. He buried his face in her neck. "We love this one, right, sweet pea?"

Her client stepped out of the dressing room, beaming. "I love it." Helen faced the ornate tri-fold mirror. "How do you do it?" The recent divorcée wore slim-fitting jeans for the first time, and she looked fantastic. "You always get it right. You're magic, Sky. Pure magic."

"Well, you're easy to work with." Skylar grinned. "You do exactly what I say."

The woman laughed. "I do. And look at the results." She turned to see her backside in the mirror. "I haven't looked like this in twenty-five years. Eat your heart out, Craig."

Her son squirmed, and if she didn't let him down, he'd pitch a fit. Seamlessly keeping up the conversation, she lowered Rocco to the floor. "Who cares what he thinks? When was the last time he made you happy? Made any kind of effort at all?"

Helen gazed into the mirror with a thoughtful expression. "I'm not sure he ever did." She drew in a breath. "You're right. You're absolutely right. I just wish…"

The woman's pain was clear in the pinch around her eyes and mouth. Skylar had suffered her own disappointment, but she'd only been twenty when her boyfriend had left her. Her experience paled next to this woman who'd raised two children and devoted thirty years to a man who'd carelessly left her for a younger woman. "You wish he hadn't turned out to be a cliché, but he did. He *is*. And now you've got a whole new future filled with possibilities. It can be whatever you want it to be." She reached for another hanger on the rack. "Okay, one more shirt to try, and then I've got the perfect dress for your date."

Helen's smile flattened. "Remember when I said I was ready to date?"

"Nuh uh. No cold feet." She watched Rocco toddle off to the bathroom. Leaving the door wide open, he pulled down his pants. *Oh, brother.* She didn't keep a potty chair in the salon's bathroom. To keep her client from noticing, though, she had to force herself not to look.

Come on, Griff. It wasn't like her brother to be late. He owned a busy motorcycle repair shop, so he always had a dozen crises to manage. Usually, though, he'd call their mom or one of their brothers to step in. He'd never left her stranded.

"I'm just thinking," Helen said. "Now that I'm looking so much better, maybe I'll meet someone at Calamity Joe's or the Tavern. I don't have to go out with a stranger I met on an *app.*"

"Except that you're only using the app to get experience, so that when you bump into the right guy, you'll be comfortable and relaxed."

Oh, God. Rocco aimed high, missing the toilet completely. Thankfully, Helen couldn't see the yellow puddle forming.

"I hate when you're right." Grabbing the blouse, her client swept the curtain shut.

Skylar tapped out a text to her brother. ***Are you almost here? I've got a client and Rocco just peed on the floor!*** Before she even hit Send, though, the salon door opened.

"Oh, thank goodness." She started forward to explain the situation but jerked to a stop when she saw it wasn't her brother. "*Jinx?*"

The big, broody guy who did custom paint jobs at her brother's repair shop was *hot.* Unruly, dark hair brushed broad, powerful shoulders, and his blue eyes had a way of studying her that said, *I wonder what you taste like.*

"I love, love, love this one." Her client came out of the dressing room and did a little twirl. The silky blouse billowed out and then landed gracefully on her hips. She stopped when she saw Jinx's imposing presence. "Oh, hello."

Giving the woman a brief nod, he said, "Hey." He scanned the room, doing a doubletake on the bathroom.

Where her son stood in a pool of urine.

God.

Before she could ask why he'd come by, Jinx headed for the bathroom. Had Griff sent him? Maybe her brother was in his truck…on the phone?

She had no idea, but she had to pay attention to her client. "Yes, I love it. It's perfect for you."

Except…what if Jinx called her son out for missing the toilet? What if he ridiculed him? Her body went hot, her skin prickly.

"Does it come in different colors?" Helen asked. "I'd love to see it in red. But, then, red might be too harsh for me. Maybe pink?"

She couldn't let Jinx humiliate her son. If he made even a single crack about missing the toilet, or if he told Rocco big boys don't pee on the floor, Skylar would kick his fine ass out—even with a client watching.

But to her surprise, Jinx dropped to a crouch, pulled up Rocco's pants, and then lifted him into his arms. Turning on the faucet, he helped her little boy wash his hands, all while chatting quietly with him.

She was disappointed in herself for assuming the worst. The single, motorcycle-riding loner had spent plenty of time around her son and had always been kind.

Not all men are going to hurt my boy.

"Unless you think I'm too old for pink?" Helen asked.

"This is just my opinion, but…" She kept an eye on the bathroom. "I think the only thing that matters is how you feel when you're wearing it. If pink makes you feel like your best self, wear it. Forget the rules or fashion advice. If you feel sexy and powerful in a shorter skirt, then wear it. You love long hair? Grow it out. It's all about empowering you. As for pink, I think with your coloring, it might wash you out, but the only way to know for sure is to try it."

Rocco's giggle filled her with warmth. With one of her hand towels, Jinx mopped up the mess, as he talked to her son and made him laugh.

She didn't know what he was doing here, but she couldn't have been more grateful for the way he'd handled the situation and treated her sweet boy.

The swish of fabric drew her back to her client. "If you want to try pink, I can find you something," Skylar said.

The faucet turned on, and Jinx washed his hands. A moment later, he dried them and reached for Rocco's hand. "Come on, buddy." He led him to the corner of her salon, where she kept a red tub filled with toys, a small white book-case, and a little art table with two child-size chairs. "Show me what you got for Christmas." Guess Griff wasn't in the truck.

Rocco, no longer grumpy, squatted as he dumped out a bag of blocks.

Which let her know he didn't have an ear infection, and he wasn't getting sick. She knew the real reason he'd been grumpy. Tomorrow, he'd leave for a week to spend time with his father's family. Eddie might have bailed on Skylar, but his parents loved their grandson and tried to spend as much time with him as they could. They didn't make too many demands, but they did ask him to attend their twice-annual family reunions. One in the summer, when the family rented a beach house in San Diego, and the other between Christmas and New Year's, when they skied in Aspen.

Rocco might only be four, but he knew what was going on. He'd seen the suitcase she'd packed. He knew he was leaving, and he hated being away from her. What could she do, though? It was the only time he saw his father.

It sucked, being a broken family.

"No, I think you're right. Pale colors do wash me out." Helen broke into a big grin. "I can hardly believe this is me."

"Well, you worked hard for it." As an image-consultant, Skylar had relationships with make-up artists, boutiques, personal trainers, and therapists to get her clients holistic makeovers. Helen had done it all. Damn right she looked good. "Okay, let's try this dress, and then I think you've got a good start with a new wardrobe."

But, instead of taking the dress, Helen's gaze remained fixed on her reflection, the joy slowly leaking out of her.

"What're you thinking right now?" These kinds of mood swings happened a lot with her clients. Reinventing yourself was an emotional experience.

With glassy eyes, she gazed at Skylar. "The thing is, he didn't just take the future I'd expected. He took my confidence."

Oh, man, Skylar knew exactly what she meant. She'd felt the same way when her baby daddy had left without a backwards glance, leaving her to raise Rocco on her own. She got up on the platform. Standing behind her client, she set her hands on Helen's shoulders. "Look at you. Craig didn't cheat on you because you're not attractive or interesting or funny or sexy or smart enough. He cheated because, when he looks in the mirror, the eighteen-year-old boy in him sees gray hair and sagging skin, and he panics. He cheated because he'll do anything to feel young again."

"That's exactly right. You don't know how much I needed to hear that."

"And we both know that the woman he's dating is only with him for the nice jewelry, expensive trips, and fancy dinners. More importantly, *he* knows that. He's willing to trade integrity for the fleeting and superficial happiness of getting to sleep with a hot twenty-something. You didn't lose weight and buy new clothes to be attractive to *him*. You did it because you're gearing up for a whole new future. Right now it hurts, but once you get a few miles down the road, you're going to be free of all the anxiety and doubt and worry that came with being his wife. You're going to be *happy*. So, try on this dress and see if it makes you feel like your best self, and then wear it tonight, so that even if it's the worst date you've ever been on, you'll know you're taking charge of your life and your future, and Craig can't impact you anymore, ever again."

Tears spilled down the woman's cheeks, and she fell into Skylar's arms. "Thank you. Thank you so much." She pulled back, swiping the moisture away. "I couldn't have done this without you. You've been so strong and positive every step of the way." Taking the hanger, she stepped back into the dressing room.

Wow. She needed this business to support herself and her son, but boy was it rewarding. The moment she stepped off the platform, she found Jinx watching her with an intensity that made her uncomfortable. He held a wooden block out to her son, who set it on a stack of them.

She wanted to shout at him, *What? Why do you always*

look at me like that? He'd been working at Griff's place for almost two years now, and he hadn't hidden his interest in her, even though she'd made it perfectly clear she wasn't dating.

When Springsteen's "Santa Claus is Coming to Town" came on, Rocco popped up, and his little butt started swishing. Laughter bubbled up at the sight. She loved seeing her boy happy. And, then, Jinx stood up and started rocking out, and Rocco dissolved into a fit of giggles.

She couldn't believe it. She'd never seen this side of the broody artist.

Jinx reached for Rocco's little hands, and the sight of this huge, inked man and her little boy electrified her heart. *This is what he needs.*

Dammit, Eddie. How could you hurt him like this?

How could you leave him to grow up without a daddy?

When Jinx grinned at her, sadness whipped instantly into anger.

Because she finally got it. Why Jinx was here.

He didn't dance. He didn't smile. He didn't joke around. He certainly didn't play with four-year-olds.

He was using her son to get a date out of her. He'd probably heard Griff say he was on his way over to babysit, and Jinx had grabbed the opportunity to win some points with her.

Well, screw him. Just as she was about to shut off the music and kick him out, her client called to her.

"Can you give me a hand?"

"Of course." She'd deal with Jinx Costello later. *You bet your ass I will.*

Nobody hurts Rocco. Not on my watch.

Stepping into the dressing room, she found the back of the dress gaping, so she zipped it up. "Look at you. You look fantastic."

"I love it. I mean…*wow*. I don't know how you manage to choose just the right things for me." Her eyes lit up with mischief. "I want Craig to see me like this. He loves the cigar bar in Owl Hoot. I want to go there with my date tonight and run into him. Let him see me." She lowered her arms. "I wish I hadn't let myself go. I wish…" She found Skylar's gaze in the mirror and let out a sigh. "I know. He'd still have cheated."

Skylar gave her a soft smile. *Looks like it's starting to sink in. Good. That means she can move on.* "I can guarantee that seeing you've lost twenty pounds and cut your hair won't be nearly as effective as seeing you living your best life. I don't know if he'll ever change, but it'll make him question his choices."

The woman gripped the hand Skylar rested on her shoulder. "I know you're right, but I still want him to see my like this." She grinned. "Okay. I'm going to get all of this. Including the shoes. I love those espadrille wedges."

"Great."

"You want to unzip me?"

"Might as well keep the dress on." She glanced at her watch. "You're meeting your date in twenty minutes."

"But I only wore my winter boots."

Skylar nodded towards the espadrilles. "You're walking one block of shoveled sidewalk. You'll be fine."

"Gah." Her hand went to her newly styled hair. "Can you come with me? I'll pay you to sit at the bar, so every time I start to panic I can look at you and get my confidence back."

"You don't need me, because you're going to talk to him the same way you do your friends when you go out to lunch. He's not a man you're trying to impress. You're not out to *win* him. You just want to meet some new people and get back into the swing of dating."

Helen let out a breath. "You know just how to relax me." She reached for the clothing, but Skylar stopped her.

"Leave it. I'll have everything delivered to your house. You just go. Enjoy your night out."

The woman grabbed her purse off a chair and stepped out into the salon. "Thank you, Sky. You're an absolute life-saver."

Skylar followed her to the door, holding it open. "Let me know how it goes."

"You know I will."

Once the woman headed down the sidewalk, Skylar shifted into Mama Bear mode. Luckily for Jinx, she'd calmed down some. Because, while he might've used her son to get to her, he'd still done a great job with him.

As she headed towards them, her anger deflated even more. It was such a perfect scene. Strings of white lights lit up her salon, making the ornaments on her Christmas tree glitter. Paper snowflakes dangled from the ceiling, twirling from the heat coming out of the vent.

Sitting cross-legged on the floor, Jinx talked quietly to her son. Rocco didn't have a huge attention span, but whatever Jinx was saying had him engrossed.

"Okay, I'm all done," she said. "Let's thank Jinx for stopping by."

Jinx handed her son a block and got up. "I thought you needed me for a few hours?"

"I've taken enough of your time. Now that my client's gone, I can manage."

"I cleared my afternoon, so I don't mind staying."

God, he was so big and…he had all this dark, intensity about him. She set her hand on her hip, so he couldn't see it was shaking. It was all such a crazy mix of emotions. He was handsome and very muscular, and he had a way of looking at her that made her feel like he'd protect and cherish her.

"I'm sure you don't." But he was too quiet, too fierce, and she didn't know what to make of him.

And now he'd used her son to get to her.

"What's that mean?"

"We talked about this." She said it quietly, so Rocco wouldn't hear. "The first time you asked me out, I told you I wasn't dating. Nothing's changed. I'm a single mother, and I work a lot of hours—not just to pay today's bills but future ones. I try to spend as much time with him while he's awake as I can, and it's incredibly hard to juggle it all."

"You don't have to do it alone."

"I don't do it alone. I have a great family, and they help me a lot, but I'm saying that I *want* to be with him as much as I can. Which puts dating on the bottom of my list of priorities. So, I'd really appreciate it if you'd respect my wishes and never use my son to get to me again."

The respect and…interest she was used to seeing in his eyes flamed out. Abruptly, he turned and went back to the play area, dropping to a crouch. "Hey, little man, I've got to go. You be good to your mama, okay?" He held up a palm, and her serious little boy slapped it.

Rocco stood there staring, as Jinx strode right past her and walked out the door.

The confusion in her little boy's eyes just about killed her. *This is why I don't date.* She couldn't bear to see him attach to men, only to have them leave. At some point, he'd just stop getting close to anyone. His heart would shut down.

The bell on the door clanged as it shut, and a blast of cold air enveloped her, as she watched Jinx head for his SUV parked at the curb. She didn't like hurting his feelings. The quiet, mysterious ones tended to be the most sensitive. Besides, even if he had used her son, he hadn't done it in a bad way. He'd made Rocco smile.

She'd been too hard on him.

Still, she'd needed to get it out there once and for all. She wasn't dating him, no matter how sweet he was to her boy. With Rocco busy stacking blocks, she pulled out her phone and called her brother.

"Hey." Griff sounded exhausted.

"Everything okay?"

"Jinx didn't tell you?" her brother asked.

Uh, no. She hadn't let him say anything. She'd just kicked him out. "Tell me what? What's going on?"

"You know that shipment of bikes that got delayed with the storm? Well, it showed up with no warning literally five minutes before I was supposed to head over to your place. That's why I asked Jinx to watch Rocco for me. He get there all right?"

A hot mix of shame and dread washed through her. "*You* sent Jinx?"

"Yeah. He pretty much raised his younger brother, so I

knew he'd be good with Rocco. Plus, he's been around him plenty of times, so it wasn't like a stranger showing up. Everything's okay, right?"

"Well, considering I just told him not to use Rocco to get to me, no, not really."

I'm such a bitch.

"Use—*what?* Where'd you get that idea?"

"He's always trying to be around me. And, when he showed up instead of you, I thought he'd convinced you to let him come over."

"Jesus, Sky, you think I'd let some guy who only wants to get in your pants watch my nephew? I love that kid like my own."

"I know. I feel terrible."

"Look, I know your ex did a number on you, but not all guys are assholes. Jinx is a good guy. Don't put him in the same trash bag as your ex."

She had done that, and she felt terrible. "I know. I'm going to call Mom and see if she can watch Rocco. I need to go apologize."

2

AFTER SPRAYING A SECOND COAT OF THE COLOR blender, Jinx set the tank aside. He'd scuff it up tomorrow, so the pearl mix stuck nicely to it.

"Jinx?" someone called.

He'd know that voice anywhere. He glanced over to find Skylar striding toward him.

Fuck me. With her platinum hair, a mouth made for pin-up posters, and the sexy swing of her hips, she knocked him off balance.

But then he remembered that he was over her.

Not to mention she'd accused him of using her son. "Yeah?"

As soon as she reached him, she lifted both hands in a gesture of surrender. "I'm sorry."

She'd talked to Griff. "Okay." He pulled the long, skinny back fender off the hanging rack and set it on the table. Running a hand over the smooth surface, he checked to make sure he didn't need to spot prime it. *Nope.* Looked ready for the gold flames.

"Jinx."

"What?"

"Can you look at me, please?"

He straightened and faced her.

"Thank you for watching my son while I was with my client. I jumped to a really ugly conclusion, and I want you to know that it has nothing to do with you. You've never given me a single reason to doubt you or not trust you, so what I said back there? That comes from me. I'm…messed up."

He got that. He didn't know the whole story, but everyone in town knew her ex had gone off to Los Angeles to become a rock star, leaving her and his son behind. That would fuck anyone up, but especially a twenty-year-old who'd just found out she was pregnant. "We're cool."

"Are we? Because I feel terrible. You're really good with Rocco. He's been grumpy all day, and you actually made him smile." She stood there, watching him.

He knew his silence made people uncomfortable, but he wasn't one for small talk. "He okay?"

"Oh, you know. It's…" She blew out a frustrated breath. "Every year, he goes to Aspen over the break between Christmas and New Year's to spend time with his father's family. He leaves tomorrow morning."

"You're not going with them?"

"Oh, God, no. And that's why he's so grumpy."

He could tell from her expression what she thought about being separated from her boy. "So, you're free this week?" Because, ever since he'd seen her with her client, he'd been working on an idea.

But before she could answer, heels clicked on the smooth concrete floor. They both turned at the same time.

Lori, in tight black jeans and five-inch high heels came sauntering over to him with a blazing white smile. In a million years, he'd never understand why such a fancy, cheerful woman would go out with him.

"Hey, there."

Her scent billowed in the air around him. He felt the twitch in his nostrils before he let out a loud sneeze.

She didn't care. Nothing got Lori Von Hausen down. She wrapped her arm around him and leaned in for a kiss. Not an air kiss, not a quick peck—no, Lori didn't do anything halfway. Cupping his jaw, she turned him toward her and planted her wet mouth on his.

Too aware of her presence, he cut a look toward Skylar —because he'd been in love with that woman for nearly two years before finally getting her message: *nope. No way in hell.*

You can fuck right off.

While rubbing the lipstick off his mouth with her thumb, Lori extended a hand toward Skylar. "Hi. I'm Lori. Jinx's girlfriend."

Girlfriend? We're just—

But before he could finish his thought, he noticed Skylar's reaction.

The feisty, spunky woman with more confidence in her pinkie than most people had in their whole bodies stood there with her jaw hanging open, shocked and…

He was going to have to say hurt, because there was no other interpretation of her expression.

He got the first part. Lori could do a hell of a lot better than his moody ass. But the hurt? That, he didn't get.

But, then, the woman he'd put down roots for reached out and shook Lori's hand. "I'm Skylar." She seemed off her mark, because after a couple beats of silence she said, "I'm Griffin's sister." She motioned, like she was trying to circulate the air. "The owner of this…shop. Jinx watched my son this afternoon, and I wanted to thank him. I'm not…he's…"

"You did?" Lori's smile faltered. She gave him a look that said, *You didn't tell me that.*

"Griff was supposed to do it," Skylar said. "But he got a shipment of bikes in." She looked to Jinx for confirmation.

He shrugged. Why would he have told Lori his plans? Griffin had asked for his help, and he'd gone.

"Motorcycles in winter?" Lori looked confused.

"For the expo in Idaho Falls." He'd already told her about that. They had a booth, and Jinx would be talking to potential customers about his designs.

"Okay, well, I should go," Skylar said. "Anyhow, I just wanted to thank you for helping out."

She started off, and his damn heart started pounding. *Don't go.*

But that was a residual response. He'd shut that door two months ago. Well, the moment Lori had walked in. "Hold up. You said you're free this week?"

Skylar nodded. "I am."

He set the rag down. "I've got a favor to ask."

She eyed him warily.

"What you did with your client? My mom could use that."

"A make-over?"

"Yeah. She's…" How did he explain? "In a rut. I've bought her things—a condo, a new car, but it doesn't change anything. She's still just going through the motions. I think what she'd really like is to feel good about herself again."

Her features softened. "Send her in. I'd be happy to work with her."

"That is *so* sweet." Lori slipped her arm through his. "You're such a great guy."

He could actually see the effort it took Skylar to tear her incredulous gaze off Lori.

"Let's set up an appointment," Skylar said. "I look forward to meeting her."

"She lives in Vegas," he said.

"Oh. Okay…are you thinking of flying her out here?" Skylar seemed confused.

"I'm not sure she'd go for it. She works long hours in the ER. Can I bring you to her?"

"You want me to go to Vegas?"

"You said you're free this week."

"I am, but I need to be here for Rocco."

He probably shouldn't push. He hadn't even pitched the idea to his mom. "Isn't Rocco going to be in Aspen?"

"Well, yes, but…"

"If anything happened, I'd fly you out to him."

"I don't know."

His mother would never ask for help, but their Sunday evening phone calls were tough on him. The exhaustion in her voice, the lack of anything in her life to talk about other than work. Not even a pet. Just work, a frozen dinner, TV, and bed. Same thing, day after day.

Now that he'd seen the effect Skylar had on her client, heard her inspiring words, he wanted that for his mom. More than he'd wanted anything in a long damn time.

He supposed, if he had a hope in hell, he'd have to tell the whole story. "My, uh, my dad was career Army." He snatched up the rag, just for something to do with his hands. "He died during his eleventh deployment. It was hard on my mom, but to be honest, she was used to him not being around. My brother, though…they were close." That familiar dark cloud loomed, threatening to engulf him, so he forced himself to think about how Skylar could help.

If anyone could get through to her, it would be this woman. "He and his buddies rode their bikes to my dad's funeral. A truck driver high on heroin mowed them down."

Lori rubbed his arm. "Oh, baby."

He swallowed past the painful knot in his throat. He never talked about his brother. Never. "We had two funerals, back to back. My mom hasn't been the same. She needs more than new clothes and a haircut." *Though, she could use both.* "The things you said to that lady? That's what she needs to hear. Will you do it?" An impulsive idea had turned into the most important thing in his life. "Please?"

Everything in her softened with compassion. "Yeah, Jinx. I'll do it. Rocco's grandparents are coming to get him at five in the morning, so I can be ready any time after that. Although, last minute tickets might cost a lot. I'll have to check into flights."

"First of all, I'm paying for everything. But, secondly, we're not flying." He grinned. "It's a road trip."

He has a girlfriend.

A gorgeous, nice, happy girlfriend.

Skylar'd had a good twelve hours to accept the fact that Jinx didn't want her anymore. That he'd found someone else. Probably someone less encumbered.

Someone who didn't constantly reject him.

Shame blazed a path down her spine. She'd been *awful* to him.

And, the thing was, he'd never been anything but kind to her. So what if he'd asked her out a couple times? Sure, he lit up when he saw her, took every opportunity to sit next to her, but he'd never pushed for anything.

And, still, she'd been a bitch—just because he'd shown interest in her.

So, it shouldn't hurt that he no longer wanted her.

She didn't want a boyfriend. Didn't have enough hours in the day to both earn a living and spend time with her son. Most importantly, she couldn't let Rocco form attachments to men who wouldn't stay.

Then why am I so upset?

Because she'd had Jinx's devotion for nearly two years, and now she didn't. And she felt like she'd lost something really, incredibly special.

With Rocco clinging to her like cat hair on a fleece jacket, she peered out the window as headlights flashed in the darkness. "Okay, sweetheart. Grandma and Grandpa are here."

Rocco squirmed, pressing hard against her as if he could slip inside a secret compartment and hide. She touched the back of his head, her fingers sifting through his silky hair. "I can't wait to hear all about snow and hot cocoa and swimming in the hot tub."

A car door slammed, and she let the curtain fall. It was time to hand him over.

Heading downstairs, she breathed in the scent of pinecones and cinnamon from the basket she'd displayed by the salon's hearth. "Everyone's going to be staying in one great, big house, so you'll get to see Aunt Carol and Uncle Jim and all your cousins."

She opened the door to find the bright, hopeful expressions of Eddie's parents. Owners of a gym, they were both fit and incredibly energetic. She didn't want to let her son go, but if she had to hand him off, she couldn't ask for more caring people. "Morning."

She'd left her son's suitcase by the door, so Mr. Ray picked it up. "Hey, kiddo."

"Morning, hon. How's our favorite little boy?" Mrs. Ray said.

Rocco kicked his legs and tucked his face into Skylar's neck. "I'll just walk him to the car." He reacted this way every time, so his grandparents were used to it.

It was brutally cold. *I should've put my coat on.* She cuddled her son closer to her body and pulled up the hood of his parka.

Mr. Ray set the suitcase in the trunk. "This everything?"

Skylar nodded, ready to hand him off, but Rocco clung to her. "Come on, sweetie."

"No." His fingernail scraped her chin, as he struggled in her arms. "I don't want to go."

Figured, the first words he'd spoken all morning, and they'd be killers. "I'm going to miss you so much, but I know you're going to have fun playing with your cousins." She reached for the handle on the car.

Rocco went nuts. "I'm not going. Mommy, *no*."

In moments like these, she hated Eddie. If he'd just stepped up to be a dad, her son wouldn't be torn apart like this. Her ex had taken a perfect canvas and slashed it with neglect.

"Hey, sweetie, look what we got for you." Mrs. Ray held out an iPad. "You can watch movies on the plane."

At that exact moment, when she was struggling to hold onto a boy who refused to part with her, when Mrs. Ray was trying to get Rocco to look at a device that meant nothing to him, Jinx's big, black SUV rumbled around the corner. His headlights flashed at them, as he pulled in behind the Rays' car.

"Let me just get him in his car seat." With a hand on Rocco's head, she ducked inside the heated car and plopped him down. As he thrashed and screamed, she kept a hand on his tummy. "Sweetheart, listen to me." He kicked her elbow. "Hey, you hurt me. Will you just listen to me for a second? Baby, everything's going to be fine. Grandma and Grandpa Ray love you very much, and they're going to take good care of you."

She knew they had a flight to catch, so she had to make this quick. As she struggled to connect the seatbelt, she vaguely heard Jinx introducing himself, the low murmur of their voices. But her focus was on getting her son situated. "I love you so much, punkin. I know this is hard for you." She blinked back tears. *Fuck you, Eddie. It didn't have to be like this.* "But Grandma and Grandpa will be with you every second, okay? You know how much fun you have with them."

The door on the other side opened, and Jinx's big body slid next to Rocco. "Hey, man."

His presence filled the car—his clean scent, fresh from a shower, and something rich and artsy—like oil paint. Rocco immediately stilled, watching him with big, wary eyes.

Jinx handed her son the iPad. "You want to see something cool? Take a look at this." When he tapped a button on his cell phone, his face filled the iPad's screen. Rocco looked from his new device to the man sitting next to him. Her son had used FaceTime before, of course, but seeing Jinx's face on that big screen seemed to impress him.

"Will you do me a favor?" Jinx asked, and her boy listened as though he were getting state secrets. "Will you show me and your mom the snowman you make?"

Rocco gave a shuddery sigh. He turned to his mom. "I'm going to make a snowman?"

She wiped the glistening tears off his rosy cheeks. "Oh, heck, yeah. A huge one. With a carrot for a nose and beets for eyes."

"And, since your mom doesn't get to go," Jinx said. "Can you show her what the mountain looks like?"

"We're going on a sleigh ride," Mrs. Ray said from the sidewalk. "It's pulled by big horses."

"You serious?" Jinx looked genuinely envious. "Ah, man. You gotta call us, okay? Let us in on it, so we can see the horses, too."

Jinx didn't sound like he was trying to sweet-talk a kid. He sounded real, like missing out on a sleigh ride was a true loss. Her son looked at Jinx in earnest and nodded. "Okay."

"Thank you, sweetheart." Skylar kissed Rocco's damp cheek and clasped the buckle on the car seat. "We'll talk every day." She leaned in to hug him and whispered in his ear, "I love you so much, my angel. So, so much." She pulled back and swept the hair off his forehead.

With glassy eyes, her son said, "Bye, Mommy."

Oh, God. Her sweet, innocent little boy. It hurt so damn much. But she knew she had to leave quickly. "Bye, angel."

Mr. Ray gave her a hug. "We'll take good care of him."

"I know you will." The only spot of comfort in this whole mess was that she knew she could count on them to care for her boy the way she would.

Mrs. Ray wrapped her arms around her. "I know this is hard but thank you for giving us time with our grandson." She pulled back, got in the car, and they took off.

Skylar stood on the sidewalk and let the emptiness consume her. The cold burned her skin. She thought about her home, how empty it felt without Rocco, and was suddenly very glad to be taking this road trip. She turned to Jinx. "You're good with him."

The sun hadn't crested the horizon, so he stood tall and imposing in the darkness, but there was something so calm about him. He tugged the scruff on his chin. "Every time my dad left on another deployment my brother had a hard time with it. Never got used to it. So, yeah, I've had some experience with it."

Up until this moment, Jinx had been a threatening entity. Now, she saw him as a man who'd suffered loss. "I'm sorry, Jinx. For your dad, your brother." In a way, he'd lost his mom, too. And she'd do whatever she could to help her —and to give Jinx his family back.

"Thanks. You got your suitcase?"

"Yes, sure." She headed back into the warm salon. "This

trip's going to be good. I always spend the week he's gone catching up with paperwork and administrative stuff, but I feel his absence so much. And I'm really looking forward to spending time with your mom."

He reached for her suitcase. "I hope I'm doing the right thing."

"It doesn't have to be a big deal. If she's not interested in working with me, then we spend a few days hanging out with her and come home. *And* we get away from the snow. No loss, right?"

"Right." She thought she saw him smile, but it was too dark to be sure. "Your in-laws seem like good people."

"They're not my in-laws. Eddie left me three days after he found out I was pregnant." She flushed the downstairs toilet, checked the dials on the oven and stove, and lowered the thermostat. "But, yes, they're really good grandparents."

Grabbing her purse, she headed back to where Jinx stood by the door with her suitcase. She didn't want to wear her parka in the car, so she pulled it off the hook and tucked it under her arm. "The thing is, I miss Rocco, and it's hard to see him freak out when he leaves me, but that's not the real issue I have with Rocco spending time with Eddie's family."

"And what's that?"

She shut off the lights, closed the door, and locked it. "They say we get our sense of ourselves from the look in people's eyes. When I look at Rocco, even when I'm frazzled or angry, I make sure he sees love. I know his grandparents show him that love, too. But Eddie resents him, and I don't ever want Rocco to look into his father's eyes and see that."

"I always liked the way you *mom*, but now I think you're

the best I've ever seen." Jinx popped the hatch and shoved the suitcase in. "You want to put anything else back here?"

As she stood there, letting his words sink in, warmth spread through her. The last five years had been one crazy ride, between Eddie's abandonment and the experience of raising a child on her own. She didn't have much that was hers and hers alone, but Jinx always made her feel special.

When he gestured to her bags, she remembered his question. She had a purse and a tote filled with snacks, a digital reader, and some magazines. She burst out laughing. "I've been a mom too long. I packed to keep us entertained in the car."

Jinx slammed the hatch closed and stepped onto the sidewalk beside her. The first rays of sunlight had pierced the darkness, and she could see his features more clearly. She'd spent so much time pushing him away, she'd missed how truly handsome he was.

Worse, she'd missed the kindness in his eyes.

He peered into her bag. "Oh, man." He pulled out a box of graham crackers. "I haven't had these in years. We used to go camping when my dad was in town. Always made s'mores."

She pulled out a six-pack of mini water bottles. "I'm such an idiot. Did I think we'd have snack time in our room?" Remembering his girlfriend, she froze. "I mean rooms. We're getting separate rooms. Obviously, we're not..." She wagged a finger between them.

"Hey, don't worry about it. Lori's cool with the trip. And, yeah, I've booked us separate rooms." He twirled his key ring around a finger. "You ready to go?"

"I am."

"Good. Let's do this." Excitement glittered in his eyes.

Her breath caught in her throat. Because for one pathetic second she'd thought he was excited to travel with her.

But, of course, she knew it was about his mom.

The hope that I can help her get her mojo back.

She knew that, and yet…they stood so close, she could see the black streaks in his light blue eyes, smell the clean of his T-shirt and something else…something particular to him that reached in and connected with her very essence. It made her heart skip a beat.

Why am I reacting to him like this?

If she had to face the truth, her response to him was exactly why she'd always pushed him away. He stirred things up, and it just wasn't the right time in her life to date.

"Jinx, I'm really glad we're taking this trip together." *I've been awful to you.* "I want to get to know you and—"

The passenger door opened and out came a boot attached to a lean, jean-clad leg. "Hey, there." Lori's voice was morning-rough, sexy.

Mortification poured over her ego like boiling water. *I want to get to know you?*

He has a girlfriend.

She struggled to compose herself. "Hey, Lori." Her too-cheerful voice sounded ridiculous.

"Everything all right?" In her puffy black parka with its fur-trimmed hood, she still managed to look sophisticated and sexy.

"Everything's great." She smiled at the woman. "Just had a hard time saying goodbye to my son."

"I'm sure." She seemed genuinely concerned. "But you're

going to have a blast. You're going to eat gross convenience store food, hit the casinos, and get drunk. All the things you can't do as a mommy."

"The fact that my immediate reaction to all those ideas was, I think I'll stay in and sleep while everyone else goes out, shows you just how much I need to do all of them. I swear, you'd never know I was twenty-five."

"Girl, you're going to have so much fun."

"You're not coming with us?" She was embarrassed at the hitch of hope in her heart.

"Nope. I already missed Christmas day with my family, there's no way I can miss the rest of this week. I just didn't want say goodbye to my sweetie-pie yet, so I hitched a ride into town just to see him off." She flashed her *sweetie-pie* a big grin. "Let's do this." And got back into the car.

His girlfriend was beautiful and vivacious and...and perfect. She didn't have stretch marks or bags under her eyes. She didn't have an ounce of bitterness in her.

Catching Jinx watching her, Skylar's body went hot with shame at thinking such stupid thoughts. "She seems great."

"Yeah, she is."

She'd never seen this softer side of him. A mix of jealousy and potent regret passed through her in a sickening roll.

You need to stop this right now.

He deserves a woman who wants him. Loves him.

And you? You had your chance, and you kicked him to the curb.

Let the man be happy.

3

As they pulled away from the curb, Lori fiddled with her phone until a song came on the speakers. "Okay with you, baby?" she asked Jinx quietly.

He just shrugged, and she leaned over and kissed his cheek. "You're such a sweetheart." Then, she twisted around to Skylar. "He's dropping me at Calamity Joe's. You want to grab a coffee before you hit the road?"

"I'd love that. Thank you."

Lori settled in her seat. "I'm going to miss you so much." She played with the hair at the back of Jinx's neck. "I wish I could come. I can't wait to meet your mom. You're such a good son."

Jinx reached for her hand and pressed a kiss in the center of her palm.

Skylar felt small and insignificant in the backseat. *Well, you can sit here and feel like a third wheel, or you can jump right in.* "Calamity Joe's has the world's best muffins."

Lori turned back to her. "Sorry, what?"

"Calamity Joe's. They make their own muffins and

scones, and they're to die-for. Dates, peaches, they put all kinds of goodies in them. Delicious." *Oh, God.*

Yep. I just used the word "goodies" with grown-ups.

Kill me now.

How 'bout we up our game here? "So, how did you two meet?" *And when?* Because she'd never seen Jinx with anyone before.

"Do you know Callie Belle?" Lori asked.

"Of course. She's a few years older than me, but she dated a Bowie all through high school, so yeah, everybody knew her." The Bowie brothers were those elusive people—insanely handsome, athletic, and confident—who seemed lightyears beyond everyone else.

"Well, I came out here to see what she was doing with her Museum of Broken Hearts. I'm in the art world, so I like to keep up with what's going on."

"Oh, what do you do?"

"I work in my parent's gallery. I'm a buyer. In fact, I came out here to check out Jackson's work."

"Jackson?"

Lori swiveled around, looking confused.

Jinx eyed Skylar in the rearview mirror. "My real name."

"I had no idea." *How do I not know that?* She'd never once thought to ask.

The moment he pulled in front of the coffee house, Lori unbuckled and got out of the car. As they headed inside, she said, "I only came out to Calamity for a visit." She grinned mischievously. "But I could be persuaded to stay."

Skylar shot a look to Jinx—were they *that* serious? But he was reaching for the door, holding it open for them.

"Have you seen Jinx's art?" Lori asked.

Skylar took her place in line. "I have. It's amazing. I've never seen anything like it."

The place was warm and smelled of cinnamon and coffee. With Calamity situated in a valley created by the Teton and Gros Ventre Mountain ranges, tourists flocked to the area for outdoor adventures. Winter was a busy season, so the coffee place was already hopping. A rowdy group of snowboarders took up several tables and chairs with their gear.

"Exactly," Lori said. "I'm so glad you feel the same way. The first time I spent the night at his place…" She cut Skylar a look. "Have you been there?"

"No." She didn't even know where Jinx lived. And, now that she knew he'd lost a father and a brother, she hated the idea that he'd been so alone and isolated these past two years.

And, suddenly, this cheerful, affectionate woman made sense. *She's just what he needs.*

"Well, the first time I spent the night, I smelled something," Lori said. "Literally, the most familiar scent in the world for the daughter of Clyde Von Hausen and Lillith Vanderburgh." She waited expectantly, but Skylar had never heard of them. "My parents are very well-known in the art world. Anyhow, I followed my nose down the hallway, and there's this bedroom—" She leaned against Jinx, and he put his arm around her. "He'd turned it into a studio and filled it with paintings. I mean, there's enough canvas in there to keep a gallery in business for a year. And I asked him if he needed my help trying to decide which ones to submit, and he goes, Submit to what?" Lori laughed, turning to the counter when it was their time to order. "I'll take the yummiest and biggest caramel macchiato you've got. Oh, and with a big ole swirl of whipped cream on top. To go, please." She looped her arm through Jinx's. "Honey?"

"Yeah, can I get a sausage and cheddar egg sandwich?"

"Sure," the barista said. "Any coffee with that?"

"Just this." He held up the water bottle he'd grabbed from the refrigerated case. "Sky?"

She didn't want him paying, so she focused on the baked goods. "You guys go ahead. I'm still deciding which muffin I want."

Jinx leaned in close, giving her a whiff of his masculine and too appealing scent. "This trip's on me. I'm paying for everything, no discussion."

She cracked a grin. "Okay, fine. I'd like a skim decaf latte and a ginger pumpkin muffin—wait, no, I think I'll try the banana chocolate chunk."

"We'll take both, please." Jinx pulled out his wallet.

The three of them stepped aside to wait for the drinks.

"Can you believe he doesn't even think about showing his work?" Lori said. "Do you know how much money he could make? Believe me, I've grown up in museums and art galleries. I recognize talent."

Skylar looked to Jinx to see what he thought of all this, but he just stood there quietly.

"I'm going to make him famous." Lori rubbed his arm. "And then he'll be the toast of the New York City art world. Right, babe?"

Fear pinched Skylar's heart. "You're leaving Calamity?"

His gaze jerked over to hers with an expression she was pretty sure said, *You care?*

And she was surprised at her own answer. *Yeah. I do.*

Why hadn't she been kinder to him? She didn't have to date him, but they could've been friends.

The barista called their names. Grabbing their cups and food, they headed over to the sugar station.

Skylar gave Jinx a soft smile. "I had no idea painting custom bikes was just a side gig."

"Oh, believe me," Lori said. "He's destined for great things. Mark my words." She tipped her head against his shoulder. "We make a great team."

"I see that." Maybe it was because she hadn't had a boyfriend since high school, but seeing their closeness hurt. She pointed to the door. "I'm going to give Rocco's grand-parents a quick call, make sure he's all right." She missed her son fiercely.

She missed a lot of things.

Like companionship. And spooning. And holding hands. And passion.

She'd held off on dating for Rocco's sake, but maybe… just maybe she was ready.

Inside the big, cleanly-swept garage, Jinx talked motorcycles with a huge, inked biker, while Skylar caught up on emails on her phone. Every now and then, the guy let out a booming laugh that totally jarred her. Blake had such a big personality, she could only smile.

The drive to Vegas was only ten hours from Calamity, but they'd left early to meet with this potential client, whose story had moved Jinx. His wife of twenty-three years had lost her battle with cancer. Apparently, the woman was so beloved in this small Utah town that five hundred people had come for her funeral.

"That's...this is what you came up with?" It was the heavy emotion in the man's voice that grabbed her attention.

She looked up from her phone to see him staring at the drawing Jinx had handed him. It was just the initial sketch. He'd told her it would go through several revisions before he painted it on the man's Harley.

"How'd you know about the dragonflies?" Blake never looked up.

"I checked out her social media pages," Jinx said quietly.

"You even got her begonias. This is...I've seen your work, that's why I reached out to you, but I never...I mean, the details..." Sifting his fingers through his long salt and pepper beard, he couldn't take his eyes off the drawing. He let out a shaky sigh.

The longer the silence went on, the more uncomfortable Skylar grew. She should leave, give them time alone, yet moving would jar the client out of this intense moment.

Finally, Blake cupped a hand over his mouth and looked away. Blinking rapidly, he drew the heel of his palm across his damp cheek. "You got..." His voice had grown thick, rougher, and he swallowed. "How'd you know about our Charlie?"

On the way down here, Jinx had told her about the defining moment in this couple's life. It had taken them ten years to finally get pregnant, and then they'd lost the baby. Blake's lips trembled, and a rush of tears spilled down his cheeks.

Jinx moved in, drawing the big man into his arms and

giving him a hug. "I got you." He tightened his hold. "I got you."

The biker nearly collapsed around Jinx, but her friend held his ground and propped the man up.

Tears blurred her vision, and sadness weighed heavily on her.

Jinx is such a good man.
I'm a damn fool.

Jinx: *You up?*

Skylar eyed the text from Jinx as she finished the last few swipes of mascara. Shoving the wand back inside the tube, she picked up her phone and took a selfie in the mirror as a response.

Jinx: *Breakfast?*
Skylar: *Yes, starving.*

She waited for more—where to meet, what time—but in typical Jinx fashion nothing came. Before this trip, his quietness had aggravated her. Now, though, it intrigued her. She wanted to know him.

She tossed the mascara into her make-up bag and then dropped it in the suitcase she'd left open on her bed. Then, grabbing her keycard, she headed out the door.

A zing of awareness shot through her at the sight of tall, dark, and tattooed Jinx leaning against the wall. He had an intense way of looking at her that stirred something dark and decadent...something she hadn't felt in a very long time.

An image flashed in her mind. Jinx lifting her and pressing her against the wall, taking what he wanted. He'd be the best kisser, she just knew it.

Damn, no wonder Lori was always touching him.

They headed toward the elevators. "You're up early," she said.

"Always."

"Yeah? Me, too, but that's not exactly by choice." She smiled to let him know she had zero resentment towards her son for the schedule she kept. She loved every minute with her baby boy. "What gets you up so early?"

"Got stuff to do."

She pressed the button. "The garage doesn't even open until eight."

"I do other stuff."

"Like?"

He hunched a shoulder. "I eat, read, paint."

"You're an interesting man, Jinx Costello." As they boarded, she remembered what Lori had called him. "So... why do they call you that?"

"Jinx?"

She nodded.

"Ah. I might need coffee first."

"Oh, I'm sorry. I don't mean to be nosy."

They were quiet for a moment, and then he said, "I like that about you."

"Like what?"

"You care. About the people in your world." He paused. "It's nice."

The doors parted, and they stepped into an active lobby. The hotel had a hot breakfast bar, but Jinx steered her outside. "Saw a diner across the street. Might be better food."

The morning was cold enough to hurt when she inhaled, but she didn't mind. The icy air cleared her mind and awakened her senses. She missed Rocco, for sure, but…she was happy to be with Jinx.

And what a surprise that is.

He had this rough exterior—the scruff, the tats, the muscles—but an incredibly sensitive soul.

They dashed across the street and entered a lively restaurant. Grabbing menus, the hostess led them to a red booth. The warmth stung her cheeks.

"Can I get you started with some coffee?" the woman asked.

"Yes," they said at the same time.

The woman grinned. "Be right back."

Jinx scanned his menu briefly, then set it down. "So… Jinx." He picked up the salt shaker, tilting it from side to side. "My brother was part of a motorcycle club, and they all had road names." His gaze flicked up to her. "I told you he died on his way to my dad's funeral."

She nodded, seeing his pain etched into the lines around his eyes and mouth. She had to check her impulse to reach for him.

"I took it hard, his passing. Dropped out of school, spent time fixing up his bike. After I painted a memorial to him on it, his friends saw it and asked me to paint their bikes. I did it, and so I hung around with them for a while." He cocked his head. "Maybe a year or so? From the beginning, they called me Jinx. It stuck. Guess they thought I was bad luck."

"Jinx…no." *God.* "What happened to you was horrible. I don't know about luck, but if that's what you want to call it, it was the worst kind. *You* certainly didn't bring it on."

The waiter flipped over their mugs and poured the coffee. "You ready to order?"

"I'd like two eggs over easy, whole wheat toast, please." Skylar handed the menu to her.

"Omelet. Cheddar cheese, peppers, onions, mushrooms." Jinx gave her the menu. "Thanks."

"You got it." She took off.

After Skylar added cream and sugar to her coffee, she held the mug in both hands, letting the warmth seep in. "I'm very sorry, Jinx. I can't believe you lost them both like that."

"My brother was the hardest. I loved my dad, of course, but my brother…"

"You were close."

"Sounds weird, considering we were only a couple years apart, but yeah. In some ways, I raised him." He glanced out the window. "I didn't want to go to college across the country, but I got a full ride to Parson's, and it seemed stupid to blow it off."

"You're not blaming yourself, are you? That he got involved in a motorcycle club?"

"I don't know about blame. I know he didn't apply to college. I know he worked in a garage, made friends with some of the guys. They became his family."

"You just feel like, if you'd been around, he'd have gone in a different direction?"

"I know he would have. I'm the one who was on his case to get homework done, meet his responsibilities. Yeah, it would've turned out differently if I'd been around." His features twisted in pain as he stared into his coffee mug. "But it's not like I should've stayed home and not gone to college. I wasn't his parent." He tugged on his scruff. "I don't blame myself, but I…" He let out a rough exhalation. "I guess it all gets tangled up inside me."

"I'm sure it does. Jinx, that's a heavy load to carry." She couldn't stand it. She reached across the table and covered his hand. "But you have to know nothing good can come out of taking the blame for something you had no control over."

"I know. You're right." He lifted his mug but didn't drink. "I just…"

"You miss him."

He set the mug down. "Every minute of every day."

"I'm sorry."

He turned his hand over, clasped hers, and the intimacy of it gave her a jolt.

She should probably change the subject. "So, after spending that year with the bikers, what did you do?"

"I guess word spread, because the offers kept coming in from all over, but I had enough projects to keep me busy. At some point, though, it was time to move on. Another club —this one in Florida—had been after me for a while, so I went there. Stayed about eight or nine months, did a lot of bikes. Might have stayed longer, but your brother called me up. Said he got requests every day for custom paint jobs, and that he was tired of saying no."

"So, you just dropped everything and moved?"

"Nah." He shook his head. "Told him I wasn't interested."

"Calamity, Wyoming, right? You'd probably never heard of it."

"Oh, I'd heard of it. But I paint motorcycles. Didn't really see how moving to a cold mountain town would be the best career move."

"But it has been? That's why you've stayed?"

His gaze snapped up to hers. For one intense moment, he froze. He looked like he'd been caught stealing money out of her purse.

The waiter leaned over with their plates, slicing through the tension. "Here you go. Can I get you anything else?"

"No, thank you," Skylar said. "This looks perfect."

"I'll freshen up your coffees."

They dug into their eggs, eating quietly for a few minutes. Long enough that her thoughts had wandered to Aspen and her son. And fucking Eddie. *So help me God if he hurts my son—*

"I think you know why I stayed." Jinx said it quietly, seriously.

A shock traveled down her spine. She didn't say a word.

"I stayed for you."

Oh, God. She hated that he'd be so direct, but also…she loved it. Loved that he put it right out there. He had a girl-friend, so it wasn't like he had an agenda. He just spoke the truth.

You can trust a man like that.

"But…" She swallowed. "I've been so mean to you."

"I wouldn't say *mean*. You've been short with me, made

yourself clear. But it doesn't matter, because I know a lot of things about you."

"Like?"

"Like you're a patient and fierce mom. I know you treat your clients the same way you treat your son—with love and respect and honesty and kindness. I know you're smart, I know you work your ass off but still stay present for Rocco. I know you've got a big, weird, loving family. I know the hurt and pain you live with and how it doesn't make you ugly and bitter. Other than not being friendly to me, I like every single thing I've seen." He wiped his mouth with a napkin. "Took me a while to get that there was nothing between us."

"It's not you." She was so glad for the opportunity to clear that up. "I've just been so…I don't know. I was going to say busy…focused on building my business and raising my son—which is true. But the thing is…" She set her fork down. "I'm angry. I don't have feelings for Eddie anymore. It's not like I want him back. It's just that it grinds through me. Rocco's growing up without a dad, and Eddie's right there. I don't understand how he lives with himself. I really don't."

"Shitty thing to do."

"And…" *Since we're being honest.* "You're a wanderer. I…" *Just say it.* "Even if I'd wanted to go out with you, I just felt like you were going to pick up and leave any minute. Move on to the next gig. I can't get involved with a man like that. It would destroy Rocco."

"That's fair. I haven't settled anywhere since I left home. But I think it's less about committing to a place or a job and more because I can't stand that I lost my brother. I can't seem to make peace with it."

"So much for time healing all wounds."

"It's more like…it'll hit me out of the blue. Zach's *gone*. Someone will be talking about their plans for Christmas, and I'll immediately think of home. I'll get an image in my head, my mom, Zach…and then it just fucking guts me when I remember he's gone, and I'll never have that again."

"God, Jinx." She slid out of her booth and walked around to his side, getting in beside him. Girlfriend or not, this man needed a hug. Wrapping her arms around him, she felt the breadth of his shoulders, the hardness of his powerful frame, and the heat from his body.

He kept his arms down, but his head tilted, his chin resting on top of her head.

She just held him—so sorry for his loss and not knowing what could ever heal him. Where her arm pressed across his chest, she could feel the rapid beat of his heart.

It struck her—he needs to make new holiday memories. *That's what will heal him.* He needs to stop wandering, fall in love, and have children, surround himself with love and the chaos of family.

And the moment she saw herself and Rocco in that portrait, she pulled away. She'd missed any chance of a relationship with this man, so it was stupid to fantasize about it. Settling back in her seat, she finished off her coffee. "Do you think Lori's your person?"

He jerked so hard he practically dropped the knife he was using to spread jelly on his toast.

Why did you say that? "Sorry. That came out of nowhere."

"No, it's…" He set the knife down. "It's new, me and Lori. It's only been two months."

"I get the feeling she's all-in."

He cracked a grin. "She's…enthusiastic."

"She's got big plans for you."

"She does."

"I didn't know you had those dreams." *Why would I? I've never given him the time of day.*

"I don't."

"Okay, I'm confused. You don't want to sell your paintings in galleries?"

"Not really. I like painting bikes. Mostly, I like the response I get. A guy comes to pick up his bike, and he breaks out in this big smile. Sometimes, he'll tear up. It hits him hard, that he gets to keep this person or this accomplishment—whatever it is he wanted painted on his bike—close, and I like that." He let out a slow breath. "Like today. That was…I wouldn't want to give that up, you know? I can't see doing anything more worthwhile with my life than that."

Happiness went bubbly under her skin. She just liked him so much. "So, you're not moving to New York?"

"No. I have no interest in living in a city that size."

She smiled. "I don't think Lori got the memo."

"Honestly, we've never talked about it. This morning was the first I've heard of her plans."

"She works there, though, right? I guess her time's running out. She's got to get back to her family's gallery."

"I guess so."

Frustratingly, he gave away nothing. Not displeasure about Lori leaving or the hope that she'd stay. She wanted to ask. She had so many questions. But she couldn't.

None of my business.

She picked up her fork and dug back into her eggs.

"Let's talk about your mom. What can you tell me about her?"

"Well, first of all…" He looked uncomfortable. "She doesn't know you're coming."

That's not good. "Because you think she's happy with her life the way it is?"

"I'm about ninety-nine percent sure she isn't happy, but she won't do a damn thing to change it."

She wished she had better news for him. "So, the thing is, my clients come to me. They *want* change. They're desperate for it. There's nothing I can do for someone who wants to keep things the same."

"Yeah, that makes sense. It's not that I'm looking for a miracle. I don't think she's going to meet you and suddenly discover a lust for life."

"What are you looking for?"

"I just want you to be around her."

She cocked her head. *Why?*

"You're a positive person. You're strong and you give off this…this energy…like anything's possible. No matter how down you are, no matter how many wheels are stuck in a ditch, you make people feel like there's a way out. Like they'll be back on the road in no time." He paused. "You did that for me." He said it quietly, almost like he didn't want her to hear.

Everything in her went soft and warm. "Jinx." Sorrow… *frustration*…sat heavily on her chest. "I wish I'd been nicer to you. You have no idea." But there was no point in dwelling on the past. "Okay, so, here's what I think. I think we don't push her to do anything. We just hang out with her and see if we can interest her in trying some new things."

He looked relieved. "That sounds good."

"What's she like? What concerns you the most?"

Hope shone in his eyes, and the table trembled from the knee jackhammering beneath it. "When I was a kid, my mom was great. She'd work all day, but when she came home, she'd make us dinner, sit with us while we did our homework. But, every time my dad came home from a deployment, they'd fight. She didn't want him re-upping, but he always did it anyway. Over time, I guess, she lost some of her spirit. There was this one fight, though, that changed her—I might've been ten, eleven? It was a blow-out. She said she couldn't do this on her own anymore, that she wanted to move back to Oregon, where she at least had family to help her. After that, she took on more hours, stopped making us dinner. She was too tired to read to Zach before bed. She stopped taking care of herself. A couple years ago, I asked her what she'd have done if my dad had left the Army."

"What'd she say?"

"That she'd wanted to work less. There's an agency that matches nurses with temporary assignments. Like, someone has a heart attack, and they need an in-home nurse for a few days. She wanted to travel. And the big thing I remember her saying is that, once he was home for good, they could finally make some friends. With Dad gone, and Mom working and taking care of us, she didn't have time to join… I don't know…Bunco groups or book clubs, whatever things married people do. She didn't have the energy to go out for drinks with her coworkers. And she really wanted friends."

Her heart hurt for this woman who'd not only lost her husband and son, but the kind of life she'd envisioned for herself. "So, maybe she's a little introverted? Plenty of single, working moms have active social lives. Maybe your dad had a big personality? She relied on him for their social life?"

First, he seemed surprised. "Yes." But then he looked mostly relieved. "That's exactly right."

"Okay, so, this is really good information. Let's not take her to casinos or clubs. We can start out in places where she can have real conversations, make meaningful connections. Now, I obviously don't know her at all, but I'm guessing she's not going to jump up and down at the offer of a make-over or a new wardrobe. But, at the same time, she could probably use both of those to see herself in a new light. She's stuck in a rut, and we have to give her a little nudge."

"Yes, to everything you just said." He slid lower in his seat. "You think this is going to work?"

"Well, the hard truth is that people don't like change. If they're doing just fine with what they've got, they really don't want to rock the boat to go after something that could end disastrously. And now, hearing that your mom's introverted, we definitely want to go at her pace and find things that will appeal to her."

"I don't think she knows what appeals to her. It's been over a decade since she's done anything. And with only five days…"

"Remember Helen, that woman you met in my salon yesterday? Her friends knew she was depressed and in a rut, so they tried to get her to do yoga, like they do, but it doesn't interest her at all, so it didn't work. So, in our initial conversations, I found out she'd played tennis in college. In fact, that's how she met her ex-husband. They were both on the tennis team, but she was better than him, and so they eventually stopped playing together. Because, yeah, his ego is that fragile. So, instead of yoga, she's back to playing tennis, and it's something she really enjoys, which means working out isn't a chore for her."

"I've tried everything I could think of. I booked a spa weekend in Palm Springs once, but she couldn't make it because of work. I thought if I bought her a car—a convertible—it would inspire her to get out more. But last time I visited I saw the car in the garage. She said it's too nice to leave it out in the Vegas heat." He glanced down at the fingers he'd clasped around his coffee cup. "Everything I've done has failed, so I'm just going to sit back and let you lead the way."

She held his gaze, something powerful passing between them. She didn't take his trust in her lightly. "We've got this."

4

"MERRY CHRISTMAS." HIS MOM STEPPED OUT OF HER condo to give Jinx a hug.

He couldn't help noticing she felt a little softer, thicker. "Mom." He hugged her a little longer, a little tighter, partly out of guilt that he'd brought someone here to change her, and partly because he was so damn worried about her.

When he pulled back, he gestured to Skylar. "Mom, this is Skylar James. A friend from Calamity."

It never failed. Even though he was dating Lori—and liked her—every time he looked at Skylar his chest got tight, his blood pumped hard, and his breath caught in his throat. When she'd hugged him in the diner, he'd thought he'd have a heart attack. It was all he could do to keep his hands to himself.

"Hello." With a grin, Skylar reached for his mom's hand, clasped it between hers. She had a way of leaning in, of looking people right in the eye, that told them they were important. "It's so good to meet you. Jinx talks about you a lot." Her voice was filled with warmth, and he wanted some of it.

Which is progress. I used to want all of it.

"Well, come on in," his mom said. "Let's get out of the cold."

"Cold?" Skylar headed inside. "Calamity's minus ten right now, so your sixty degrees is downright balmy."

"Let me take your coat." His mom held her hands out for Skylar's parka.

Jinx looked around the condo. With the blinds shut, the condo looked tired and gloomy. Other than a couple of his paintings hanging on the walls, the room had no personal touches. "Hey, Mom, no tree?"

"No." His mom leaned into the closet to hang up the coat. "It's just me here. I didn't want to bother."

"You used to love Christmas." He thought of Skylar's salon, the twinkling lights, the smell of pine and cinnamon. The feeling of home. In contrast, his mom's place felt stark. Like she was a traveling salesman just passing through.

His heart twisted at his mom's isolation. He hoped like hell Skylar could help her. She needed friends, hobbies, interests.

His mom turned to face them. "I loved it when you were guys were little. Now, there's really no point."

"If you love Christmas and don't want the bother, you should come to Calamity next year," Skylar said. "We go all-out. Lights everywhere, a huge tree all lit-up in the town green. The coffee shop rolls out a cart and sells hot cocoa. We've got carolers. It's awesome."

"That sounds lovely. Maybe I will come." She jerked her

thumb towards Jinx. "Of course, it all depends on whether he's still around."

"I'll be there."

His mom looked surprised. "You're staying?"

"I am."

His mom eyed him thoughtfully. "I'm glad to hear it." She rubbed her hands on her scrubs. "Well, I just got home and haven't had a chance to go shopping, but I can make you some sandwiches. Anyone hungry?"

"We just ate, Mom. We're good."

"I'll bring out some drinks."

"Just water for me, thank you," Skylar said. "Can I help?"

"No, no. I'll just be a second." His mom practically ran into the kitchen.

Troubled, Jinx watched her go. "She doesn't want us here."

"She's used to being alone," Skylar said. "Visitors mess with her schedule."

"I'm her *son*." Anger cracked in his voice. It surprised him, and he quickly looked away.

"I'm sorry. I shouldn't have called you a—"

"No, it's not you. It pisses me off that she doesn't want to spend Christmas with me. She chose to work on the twenty-fifth. Told me to come after, if I wanted to visit." *Yeah, if I wanted to visit. Not that she wanted me to come.*

He sounded like a whiny little boy, when all he wanted was to get his mom's mojo back. It just had been a long time since his mom had loved him. When he'd lived at home, she'd taken care of his basic needs, but the days when she'd spent any real time with him…touched him with affection…were long gone.

"It isn't personal." Skylar gestured around the bland room. "I think she's in survival mode. Routine helps her with that."

She came up close, and his body felt her nearness like a jolt of static electricity. The hairs on his arms stood on end, and a shiver ran down his spine.

"What do you bet she has her frozen dinners stacked according to days of the week, and she's waiting to watch her favorite show tonight at eight?" Skylar gave him a reassuring smile. "One thing I can say for sure, I've never had a client who didn't wind up in a better place."

A moment later, his mom came back with two glasses full of water. She handed one to each of them. "So, if Christmas in Calamity's so great, what brings you to Vegas?"

He shouldn't be hurt. He *wouldn't* be. Everything Skylar had just said made perfect sense. "I wanted to spend it with you." *Don't you want to spend it with me?*

I'm all you have left.

"That's sweet. Thank you." She gestured for them to sit on the couch, the same she'd had his entire life. "So, Skylar, what do you do?" She brought over a dining room chair and sat across from them.

"I'm an image consultant."

"What's that, exactly?"

"I know. Weird job, right? Okay, so, for example, when a woman's graduating college and ready to go on her first set of interviews, she might come to me so we can put together a look. Not just clothes but hair and make-up, too. I have a lot of divorced women looking to reinvent themselves. Some want to start dating but most just want to find out who they are again. Their identities have been lost in their family's lives."

"Sounds interesting." She cut him a look. "You're not hoping I'll reinvent myself, are you?"

Yeah, she'd figured it out. "I want you to be happy, Mom. That's all."

She turned back to Skylar. "Jackson should've checked with me first, before you came all the way out here and missed out on the holidays in your town. I'm not looking to revamp my image. I'm not going to date or change jobs."

"Mom, it's not about dating." *I'm sitting on the same couch Zach peed on when we were watching Toy Story.* Whatever wave of hope he'd ridden the last twenty-four hours crashed on the shore of reality. Because what Skylar had told him that morning in the diner was true.

His mom wouldn't change, because she didn't want to. And there wasn't a damn thing he could do about it.

Because his family had been irrevocably shattered.

"What is it you want from me, Jackson?"

He was tired of being careful with her. He got up and yanked the pull cord on the blinds. Sunlight streamed in. "I want you to make friends. I want you to date, travel, get out of this condo and have some fun. You've worked hard your whole life…I'd like to see you happy."

"I live in the desert, so the blinds are going to stay closed during the hottest part of the day. And, honestly, Jackson, I'm on my feet and around people all day long, so when I get home all I want to do is eat, read, and sleep. I need the income, so I can support myself into old age. So, there's not going to be a big social life or travel. I'm sorry my life upsets you, but I'm fine."

"Why is fine good enough?" And that was it right there. Before he'd met Skylar, he'd been fine, too.

He remembered it so clearly. The minute he'd looked into her eyes he'd felt this *pop*. It was hard to explain, but it had snapped him wide awake. He could've sworn he'd heard a voice in his head that said, *That's her. That's the one.*

From that moment on, fine had not been good enough. "There's more for you, Mom. There's better. And you deserve it." He wasn't all that great at communicating, but he realized it mattered a whole hell of a lot. "I think...I think Dad stole something from you."

His mom's eyes flared with surprise.

"He stole your power. For years, I watched you fight him, demand that he get out of the Army and come home. But he didn't listen. He didn't care what you wanted and eventually you gave up." He sat back down on the edge of the cushion, elbows on his thighs, and looked right into her eyes. "You gave up. I brought Skylar here because I've seen her with her clients. I've seen her help them get their power back. I've seen her client cry because Skylar made her feel so good about herself. I want that for you."

His mom watched him for a moment, eyes filled with sadness. "You're right. He did do that." Defeated, she looked to Skylar. "What do you want me to do?"

"Not a thing. I told Jinx, and I'll tell you, people come to me because they're not happy, they need to make some changes. If you don't want to do that, then let's just hang out in Vegas. We're here for five days. Let's have some fun."

. . .

Jinx dreaded this conversation, but it had to be done.

He got that Lori felt possessive around Skylar—he had no doubt he was shit at disguising his feelings for her. But *I could be persuaded to stay* was something more.

He glanced at his phone, waiting to hear back from her. This conversation was going to suck. But it couldn't be helped. He had to do it.

Because being around Skylar did things to him that shouldn't happen to a man dating another woman.

They'd spent all day and night checking out casinos and walking the strip. They'd visited the aquarium and the fountains at the Bellagio. After dinner and a show, they'd dropped his mom off and come back to the hotel.

And every minute with Skylar had been physically painful. His feelings for her hadn't gone away. In fact, they'd come roaring back. Neither he nor his mom were big on conversation, and Skylar had known just when to be quiet and when to engage. She'd asked questions and listened to the answers.

A memory slugged him, and he closed his eyes to fully experience it. They'd been walking through the tunnel, when a shark had come right up to the window. Startled, Skylar had taken a step back and fallen right against him. Jesus, she'd smelled so good—something floral and feminine—and he'd felt a pulse of electricity on his skin. Without even thinking, he'd wrapped an arm around her and…he hadn't let go.

Worse, she hadn't pushed away.

For one long moment, he'd gotten to know what her body felt like against his—and it had been bliss.

This isn't good. He couldn't go back to the torture of wanting a woman he couldn't have.

Too late. There was just something about her. She made him think about his future in a way he'd never do with Lori.

Well, it made him think about a lot more than his future.

It made him think about sex.

About her walking into his room with sultry eyes that told him exactly what she wanted—and what she wanted was him. Her body hot, pliant. Her arms reaching for him, wrapping around his neck.

About filling his palms with her breasts, pushing them together, feeling the heavy, soft weight. Trapping his cock between their bodies and grinding against her stomach.

Fucking her against the wall in his hotel room.

Pleasure spiraled through his body, leaving him hard and frustrated, with no outlet.

At the restaurant tonight, he'd had to curl his fingers into a fist to keep from grabbing her thigh under the table and sliding his palm up high enough to see if she wanted him as much as he wanted her.

Did she want him?

She'd sure as hell been a lot nicer to him.

And, sometimes, he thought she'd looked at him with longing. With…lust.

Or maybe he was making shit up because he wanted her so fucking badly.

He needed to talk to Lori.

He texted for the third time. ***Need to talk. You around?***

She'd always responded to him right away. She liked to

text him throughout the day to let him know she'd been thinking about him.

Lori was...*she's amazing.* Cheerful.

But she's not mine.

His phone vibrated. *Lori.* "Hey."

"Hey." She sounded down. A first for her.

"I haven't heard from you. Everything all right?"

"Not really." She let out a huff of breath. "I'm being stupid. I keep seeing the pictures Skylar posts on social media, the three of you together, and I'm jealous."

He'd been careful about that, always putting his mom between them so he wasn't touching Skylar. He didn't want to hurt Lori.

But I'm going to.

"*I* want to be there with you," she said. "I want to meet your mom and be the one to take her shopping and get her a make-over."

He figured she wanted him to say she could come with him next time. But he couldn't give her that. "Lori—"

"I mean, Skylar's from Calamity, you know? She comes from a small cowboy town. You probably need someone a little more worldly, someone who knows fashion."

What? That's not what we're doing here at all. "It's not about fashion. I don't care what clothes my mom wears as long as they're not the same ones she wore twenty years ago. I want her to try new things, make friends. I want her to feel better about herself." He paced to the window, pulling aside the curtain. "Walking around Vegas today drove it all home. My mom took us to all the tourist attractions, and when I asked if she knew of any interesting places to go, she said she didn't. She hasn't even been to the Hoover Dam. It just reinforced that she hasn't explored this city at all. She doesn't leave her damn condo."

"Well, I've been thinking. What if I fly out there for New Year's? Forget driving Skylar back. We'll get her a flight, and you and I can have a long weekend in Vegas. I can bring your mom some clothes and jewelry from the city. Can you imagine her face when she opens up presents from Gucci and Burberry? I could get her some scarves, a handbag. Get me her sizes, and I'll go wild."

Jinx leaned against the window, looking down at the bright lights and flashing neon signs of the Strip. "No, don't do that."

"No, don't come out there? Or, no, don't buy her designer things?"

"I don't want you to come out here." In the silence, his skin prickled. He hated hurting her. She was a great, positive person. "Lori, I like you a lot. You're fun and smart and beautiful, but we're not on the same page."

"Page? What does that even mean? What page am I on?"

"You're talking about showing my work, and me moving to Manhattan."

"Well, I mean, we can show your work on the west coast, but I think your best chance for a great launch is in the city. But I was thinking—and I actually brought it up with my parents—what if I started a gallery in Owl Hoot?"

The town, a living museum of the late Eighteen-hundreds gold rush days—had an upscale resort and spa. An art gallery would be a good addition to the lobby's shopping arcade.

Just…not one run by her. "That's—no, Lori. I don't want you to do that."

"I don't think you realize how talented you are."

"I like what I do. I like working in the garage with everybody around me. I like talking to the clients and hearing their stories, and I really like seeing their faces when I bring their stories to life on their bikes."

"Okay, you can still do that, only it wouldn't be motorcycles. It would be real art. We could do commissions only, where you'd meet the client, hear their story, and create a piece based on that. How cool would that be?"

"Lori." He let out a breath. "I'm not moving to New York, and I'm not changing my work."

"But you're so talented. You don't understand how important your work is."

"But that's the point. I do understand how important it is. It's important to everyone who hires me to paint their bikes. Listen, the point isn't about art or moving. When I said we're not on the same page, I meant with our relationship. I think you're a few steps ahead of me."

She sucked in a breath. "You don't see a future with me?"

I only see Skylar James. She's in my blood and my tissue and fibers. "No," he said quietly. "I don't."

"Then what have we been doing?"

"Dating. We've known each other two months, and we've gone on seven dates."

"But who's keeping count, right? Jackson, I'm thirty years old. I've had enough boyfriends to know—when I finally meet the right guy—that he's the one."

"I'm not the one, Lori." He said it as gently as he could.

"This is about her, isn't it? I knew it. I saw it in the pictures."

"Saw what?"

"When you were at the fountains, Skylar took a picture of you and your mom. And your mom's all amazed at the show, but you're just standing there staring at Skylar. I could see it on your face. You're in love with her."

"I'm not ending things with you because of another woman. I'm ending it because I don't feel the same way you do."

"No, it is her. I see the way you look at her. God, Jackson, how can you choose her over me? She has a kid. Do you really want to be a father to some kid who's not yours?"

"You're jumping ahead. Skylar's not interested in me. She made that clear the moment I met her. I'm talking about us. We want different things, and I'm not in this with you."

"Are you seriously breaking up with me?"

"I am. I've had a great time with you, but we just don't want the same things."

"I need to go."

"I'm sorry, Lori. I don't want to hurt you."

"Well, you did."

After she disconnected, he tipped his forehead to the cool glass. While he was glad it was done, he hated that he'd left her so unhappy. He'd honestly had no clue she'd envisioned a life for them in New York.

He'd like to say breaking up with Lori had cleared the way for a relationship with Skylar, but that wasn't true. He was back to being alone.

Lori had pulled him out of his isolation. Funny thing, he'd told her he liked working with people in his garage, as opposed to being alone in a studio, but he'd never gone out for drinks with the others. For the first few months he'd worked there, he'd gotten nightly invitations to join them. The offers had dwindled, and now everyone left him alone.

Just like he'd wanted.

Just like Mom.

A knock on the door startled him out of his thoughts.

He hoped like hell it was Skylar, but he knew better. The moment they'd stepped off the elevator, she'd practically raced to her room. She couldn't wait to get away from him.

Peering through the peephole, his heart about exploded when he saw that short, platinum hair. Flinging the door open, he said, "Hi." Too excited, he tried to calm down. "Hey." He stepped aside to let her in.

"You okay?"

"Sure. What's up?" The question came out so curtly, it had to have sounded like he didn't want her here. "Come in."

Watching him carefully, she headed into his room "You seemed disappointed with how things went today, so I wanted to check in with you."

"I did?"

"Yeah. You didn't seem to have fun at the shark reef or the fountain or the restaurant or the show...."

"I had a great day. I guess I was disappointed that she's lived here for five years and still doesn't know her way around the city. She left Arizona to get away from the memories, but the only thing she changed is her zip code."

A devilish grin lit up her eyes. "You trust me?"

He didn't even have to think about it. "Completely."

"I needed a day to get to know her. Here." She handed him a piece of paper. "Tomorrow's itinerary. If you don't like anything on here, let me know, and I'll make some changes.

But all day, I had these ideas for things to do, and I couldn't wait to get back to the room to book them."

"And here I thought you couldn't wait to get away from me."

"What? No." Her cheeks burned red. "Of course not."

He glanced down at the list but didn't bother reading anything. He didn't care. He was just really fucking glad to hear she hadn't run from him. Even happier to feel the energy crackling between them. "Thanks."

"Hope you've got room on your credit card, because we're going to have fun tomorrow."

"Don't you know?"

"Know what?"

"When it comes to—" He caught himself before he said, *You.* "My mom, anything goes."

She stood there in baggy pajama pants with little Santas all over them and a long-sleeve red T-shirt, and she was the sexiest woman he'd ever seen. He loved how her short hair let him see her whole face. It made her light brown eyes pop and accentuated the mouth he ached to kiss.

"Big spender, huh?"

"I live alone in a studio apartment over Mr. Takashi's garage. I don't have many expenses."

"Makes it easier to pick up and move onto the next town, huh?" She said it playfully, but he knew she was testing him.

And, if he had a hope in hell with this woman, he would not fail. "I'm not moving on. I'm staying in Calamity." He gestured to a set of chairs in front of the window. "You want something to drink? I bought some waters from the gift shop."

"No, thanks. I'm about to go to sleep."

Still, she didn't go. He didn't mind. He could stand here and talk to her all night long. He liked the sound of her voice and the way she was always pressing her hand against her collarbone, gently, just resting it there. It drew his attention to the lack of rings on it.

He'd like to put one on the finger next to her pinkie.

A jolt of energy blasted through him. The startling truth of it: he wanted to marry this woman. *That's how sure I am about her.* He'd be a dad to Rocco, and he'd get to wake up to her beautiful face every day for the rest of his life.

Determination seized him. *I want her.*

And I'm not going to give up. "How's Rocco doing?" There wouldn't be anymore Loris. He'd wait as long as it took to win over Skylar James.

"He's good. Eddie bailed on the trip, so that eliminates that worry. Everyone else in the family loves Rocco. So, now, I can really enjoy myself." She headed to the door. "Be ready, painter boy. Tomorrow's going to be a blast."

5

JINX SAT ON THE BLEACHERS, THE BILL OF HIS BALL CAP shielding the sun from his eyes. The roar of engines filled the brisk air, and his ass hurt from sitting so long on the metal bench, but he didn't care.

Because he was happy.

It was only eleven in the morning, and already Skylar had knocked it out of the park.

For breakfast, she'd taken them to the Porter House Arboretum, a magnificent indoor garden—considered the largest greenhouse in the world. Landscape designers rented plots to display their skills, creating settings filled with flowers, hedges, trees, and fountains. The opposite of Vegas, the place was quiet and peaceful and hosted various clubs like book, bocce ball, chess, dominoes, and poker.

Right there, while they'd had breakfast at the café, his mom had left them to go join a gardening class and the book club. *Fuck, yeah.*

And now…this? *Brilliant.* "How did you know?" Jinx watched his mom race the Maserati around the track.

"The whole time we were walking around yesterday and last night, she noticed every flashy car that passed us by. When that Porsche came tearing around a corner, she said something like, 'I like the way the air-cooled 911s purr,' and I thought, Okay, we're getting this woman behind the wheel."

The moment his mom had pulled off her helmet after the first session, he'd known Skylar had found something important. His mom's eyes had glittered with excitement. Who knew this woman who lived in scrubs and ate frozen dinners would be a speed demon? Right on the spot, he'd paid for a second one.

He couldn't have been more impressed with Skylar. "You pay attention."

"It's different for me. She's not my mom. You're worried about her."

"Nah, it's different perspectives. I'm looking for what's wrong. You're looking for what interests her." All these years —the wasted vacations and gifts. "I feel like an asshole."

"Oh, cut it out. You're a great son. We're only here today because you never gave up." She leaned against him—just a touch of shoulders—and he stopped breathing.

He got a hit of her sweet, feminine scent and a view into the V-neck of her blouse, revealing the swells of her breasts. Need roared through him, making him embarrassingly aroused.

If she were his, he'd let her know every day of her life how beautiful and wanted she was.

"So, tonight...what made you pick this particular club we're going to?" His mom didn't like loud music or dancing or any kind of night life.

"Every time we passed by a club, she did this." She winced and closed her eyes.

He smiled. "That's exactly what she does."

"But do you remember when that limo pulled up outside the Bellagio and those older couples got out?"

"You mean the men in suits? And that woman in a dress that…" He motioned behind his neck.

"Yes, the halter dress. It had a cinched waist and a full skirt, and the women looked old school glamorous. Maybe I'm crazy, but I thought I saw something in her eyes—something like longing."

"You're not crazy." A memory hit him. "Sunday used to be the day we cleaned house. From the time I was old enough to hold a duster, I had chores. My mom would put on music, and the three of us would clean." He'd forgotten about that. "It didn't feel like cleaning. It felt like the three of us doing something together. I remember her playing Frank Sinatra and Dean Martin. Songs from that era." Another memory came. "And she liked Gene Kelly movies. She watched the classics." Jesus, how had Skylar picked that up about his mom? "I can't believe you caught that from one look."

"I'm so glad to hear that. She's going to love this place." Skylar grinned. "Right after she's done here, let's take her shopping. We'll get her something glamorous to wear. I think, once she sees herself in the mirror, she's going to notice that she hasn't trimmed her hair in a long time. And her complexion's a little dull."

He wanted to haul her into his arms and kiss the fuck out of her, but since he couldn't do that, he took a chance and wrapped an arm around her. "You're magic, Skylar James. Pure magic."

And, to his great surprise, she didn't push him away. She stayed tucked within the shelter of his body.

Skylar flipped through the dresses on the circular rack, not seeing anything she thought Amanda would like. Most of them were too flashy.

"You like this one, Mom?" Jinx held up a green, cap-sleeve dress with a Peter Pan collar.

His mom, instead of looking for clothing, stood in the center of the high-end boutique watching a recording of her driving. She glanced at the dress. "That's lovely. I'm not sure about the color, though." Turning back to her phone, she shook her head. "That was amazing. Thank you, Jackson, Skylar. Today was…" She let out a breath of pure satisfaction. "Perfect."

Skylar shot a look to Jinx and loved the happiness she saw in his eyes.

I love my job. Honest to God, there was no greater joy than helping a woman find her way back to her best self.

"I'm glad, Mom."

"It was exhilarating," Amanda said. "I want to do it again."

"We could go back tomorrow." Jinx looked eager, hopeful. "Anything you want."

"And the arboretum," Amanda said. "I didn't even know it existed. All that greenery in the middle of the desert." She grinned. "I can't wait for my first gardening class."

Jinx's expression was full of awe, and all Skylar could do was smile.

The next step was to find a way for Amanda to turn a day of fun into a lifetime of activities she could pursue. Abandoning the rack, she said, "I was talking to the manager at the racetrack, and he said there's a company here that hires test drivers."

"Really?" Amanda looked to her son for confirmation. "That's a thing?"

"It sure is," Skylar said, since Jinx hadn't been there for the conversation.

"What kind of cars?"

"Supercars. Just like you drove today. He said the company's based here because of the miles of open road out here in the desert. I took his card, if you're interested." She pulled it out of the interior pocket of her purse.

"Are you serious?" Amanda plucked the card out of her fingers. "I'm very interested." She read the words, as though they held the cure to healing a broken heart.

Scanning the boutique, Skylar noticed some dresses at the back of the store that were less sparkly. She hoped to find something close to the image she had in her head. Jewel tone, a full skirt…she really thought that would appeal to Amanda.

"What about this one?" Jinx held up a dark red maxi dress. It had a pleated skirt and a fitted top with a sweetheart neckline.

"That's it." Skylar hurried over. "You found it." She grinned up at him, and the world fell away. His smile dazzled her, and suddenly he didn't feel like some guy. He felt like a man she knew well.

He feels like mine.

It both thrilled and terrified her at the same time.

Men leave.

No, Eddie left.

She had to wipe out that ugly voice once and for all. Jinx…he was strong, loyal, stable, kind, generous. He was nothing like Eddie.

Amanda touched the skirt, lifting the accordion-style fabric. "Oh, I don't know."

Skylar tore her gaze away from Jinx to focus on his mom. Immediately, she could see the woman's struggle. She wanted it—no doubt about that—but she wasn't ready to take that step. The purchase of a simple dress seemed like standing on the precipice of a new life.

"You don't like it?" Jinx asked.

"No, I do. But it's too expensive. I'm only going to wear it once."

Jinx held it out to her. "Mom. It's my gift to you."

"I have plenty of dresses at home. Besides, the racetrack was more than enough. Let's go home and rest a bit before we go to dinner."

In his quiet, thoughtful way, Jinx took a moment to consider. As much as she wanted to help him, she knew this issue was between mother and son.

While he considered, Amanda's finger ran along the collar of the dress.

"My job pays well," Jinx said. "And I don't have a lot of expenses. It makes me happy to do nice things for you. It'll make me feel good to know you have a bunch of new clothes that make you happy." He leaned closer to his mom. "Let me do this for you."

"Okay." His mom's tone remained uncertain.

The salesclerk swung by. "This, too?"

Jinx handed it over. "Yes."

"Okay, let's see." Skylar glanced around the small store. With its patterned red wallpaper and crystal chandeliers, it looked like the boudoir of a dancer from another era. "We have blouses, pants, and a couple of blazers." *That's enough for now.* "You ready to start trying them on?"

Amanda looked to her son for confirmation. It wasn't about money. Maybe clothing felt too personal. *Like, if you owned nice things, you'd have to wear them.*

You'd have to be a different person.

"Okay," Amanda finally said, and both Skylar and Jinx relaxed.

They followed her to the curtained dressing room and sat beside each other on a velvet love seat. Skylar reached for Jinx's hand and squeezed, surprised by his eager, powerful grasp. "We'll be right out here," Skylar called. "Come show us your favorites." She glanced over at him, his fierce expression getting her all riled up. God, she wanted to climb on his lap, scrape her fingernails across his scalp, and find out what a kiss from Jinx Costello felt like.

"Thank you."

That mouth. She heard his words, but she read *I'm gonna fuck you so hard* in his eyes. "You're welcome. I'm…" *This is crazy.*

Cut it out. You're here for his mom.

He has a girlfriend.

The reminder dumped a pot of cold water on her libido. And, yeah, it sucked that she'd missed her shot with him, but maybe this trip—what she'd done for his mom—made up for the way she'd treated him.

"I'm happy to be here." Her voice came out as dry and scratchy as sandpaper.

When his tongue came out and licked his bottom lip, she watched it, aware of the tingly sensations running down her spine and pulsing between her legs. The way her heart thundered, and desire blossomed across her skin told her she felt something very different from happy.

She was attracted to Jinx in a way she'd never felt before. *This is why I pushed him away.*

Because it scared her half to death. Eddie had been her first love, and when he'd abandoned her, he'd broken more than her heart. He'd shattered her ability to trust.

But Jinx was a man. A once-in-a-lifetime kind of man. She could love him in that profound, in-sickness-or-in-health kind of way.

Which meant…he could destroy her.

He's worth the risk.

And right then she knew it. If things didn't work out with Lori, if he ever wanted to give her a second chance, she would absolutely, whole-heartedly take that risk.

When gratitude left his expression, when color rose high in his cheeks, when his gaze drifted down to her mouth, she knew he'd read every emotion in her heart. She released his hand. "Sorry."

"For what?"

"Your girlfriend won't appreciate me touching you. I know I wouldn't want to see another woman's hands on you."

He took her hand back. "We broke up."

Her body went hot. The clash of excitement and fear made her sick to her stomach. "You…what? Why? When?"

"Last night. Right before you came to my room."

"But why? She's so nice and…happy."

"Yeah, I know. That's why I dated her. She came out of nowhere…pulled me out of my cave, but I never caught feelings, you know?"

This weird, weightless feeling came over her. She wasn't on the couch anymore. She was hovering, hope beating a painful drumbeat in her heart. Thoughts floated, but she refused to pull them in, to let them settle long enough to read them. *Is this happening?*

Could he be coming back to her? She reached for the armrest to keep her grounded.

"And I guess being around you really drove that home."

Happiness hit like a punch to the chest, knocking her back. Tears burned, and she couldn't explain it. It made no sense. "You…have feelings for me?"

"I think you know I always have. It's cool. I know you're not into me. But it's there for me, and I can't pretend it's not. So, I ended it. It's not fair to be thinking of one woman when you're with someone else."

She could barely speak past the emotions hurtling through her. "She must be devastated." Her voice sounded scraped raw. A hot tear spilled onto her cheek.

He reared back. "Oh, Jesus. I didn't mean to upset you."

She shook her head. "You didn't. I'm just…" An army of fire ants marched through her body. She was stinging, burning…and… "I'm scared."

"Of me?" He looked appalled.

"No, no." She swiped the tear away. "Of this. Us."

He leaned in close. "Why? Why does it scare you?"

"God, Jinx. Because it's big, this thing. We're—"

The curtain swished, and Amanda stepped out of the dressing room in a teal-colored short-sleeved swing dress. The belt showed off a trim waist and the flare of her hips. She turned to face the mirror. "Oh. I don't know where I'd wear something like this." Excitement radiated off her. There was no hiding how much she loved the dress.

"It looks great on you, Mom. We're getting it."

Amanda's eyes sparkled. "I don't have shoes or…jewelry." Her hand went to her hair. "I can't remember the last time I had a cut." She turned to them. "I don't *need* this dress. I have something I can wear tonight."

Jinx squeezed Skylar's hand and got up. "You like it?"

Amanda couldn't take her eyes off her image in the mirror. "Yes," she whispered.

"Then, get it," Jinx said. "And anything else you tried on that you liked."

Skylar hopped up. "Dinner's not until eight, so we have plenty of time to get shoes and jewelry. And, if you're interested, I asked about the salon in my hotel, and they take walk-ins."

"How're you doing?" the clerk said, as she approached. "Oh, that looks fabulous. It's made for you."

"It really is," Skylar said.

Amanda looked to her son, and Jinx gave her a single, deep nod.

"Okay." Amanda's tone said, *This is out of my control. I'm just going along with these crazy people.* "I'll get it."

"Great. Anything else?" the clerk asked.

"I've got a few more things." Amanda gestured to the

dressing room. "But I'd like to look at shoes and jewelry for the dress. My son's taking me dancing tonight."

The clerk smiled. "I've got just the pair of heels to go with it. You're going to love them. Come on, let me show you."

Skylar started off after them, but Jinx grabbed her wrist and hauled her back.

"We *are* big." His intensity thrilled her. "But you can count on me. You can trust me, Skylar."

———

As Jinx pulled into his mom's condominium complex, she said, "She's lovely."

He glanced at her, unused to that soft voice. "Skylar?"

Her mom nodded, curiosity in her eyes. "Is there anything there? I mean, I know you're seeing someone else, but the chemistry between the two of you is off the charts."

"I broke up with Lori."

"Oh, I didn't know."

"Yeah. Last night."

"Because of Skylar?"

"Because I…" *Because it's big this thing, us.* He couldn't believe she felt it, too. He wouldn't let his hopes get too high, though. He could've misunderstood. She could've meant something else entirely. "Yes, because of Skylar. I've been in love with her for two years. She never gave me the time of day."

"Until now."

"I don't know, Mom." He pulled into a parking spot right alongside his SUV.

After the boutique, they'd gone back to the hotel. Oddly, Skylar hadn't come to the hair salon with them. Said she'd had a few errands to run. He'd given her the keys to his car and hadn't heard from her since.

But she was back at his mom's place, and he couldn't wait to see her.

When he met his mom in front of her car, she stopped on the sidewalk and pressed her hand to his forearm. "I do. I see the way she looks at you—and it's a mix of…honestly? She looks at you with awe. Like she can't believe you're real. But, also, there's fear there. I don't know her story—only that she's a single mom—but I think you need to be careful with her. If you can do that, I think you two could have something special."

"I don't know what she wants."

"Ask her. If you've learned anything from watching your parents, it's that you have to listen to each other. Ask her what she wants and always, *always* find ways to compromise."

He could hear how important it was to her, so he said, "I will." But she didn't know that he'd wait as long as necessary, and he'd give Skylar whatever she needed to feel safe with him. He wasn't going anywhere.

They headed up the stairs to his mom's unit. Before unlocking her door, he turned to her, taking in the stylish haircut, the warm chestnut color, and the professional make-up job. "You look great, Mom." Sophisticated, elegant. "I didn't bring Skylar here because I think you're not beautiful enough. I don't care how you dress or whether you blow dry your hair. I just want to see you living again. That's all."

"I know that, I do. And even though I resisted, I'm actually amazed at what a good haircut and some make-up can do for my attitude. I feel…" She grinned. "Pretty badass."

He opened the door, and they both reared back at the strong scent of cinnamon and pine.

"What's going on?" His mom pushed past him.

Skylar had transformed the place. A Douglas Fir took up one corner of the room, tinsel and ornaments glittering in the multi-colored string of lights. She hadn't seen them enter, as she stuffed wrapped presents inside the stockings she'd rested on top of the squat entertainment center.

Her ass shook as she sang along with Chuck Berry's "Run Rudolph Run." When she leaned over to pick up another present, she cut a look to the doorway and jerked up. "*Oh.*" She shut off the music. "You scared the bejesus out of me."

Late afternoon light spilled into the room, and everything looked so damn cheerful.

"What have you done?" His mom touched the garlands hanging off the curtain rod.

Skylar hugged the present to her chest. "Is this all right? I wanted to surprise you."

"But Christmas is over."

"Oh, if you're worried about the cost, I got this tree from a man who was clearing out his lot. He gave it to me for free. And the ornaments are all from CVS. They were seventy-five percent off. But, I mean, you can store everything for next year." Her gaze slid to his with a grimace that said, *Did I mess up?*

But his mom rushed over to her, throwing her arms around her. "Thank you, Skylar. This is wonderful. I would never have done this for myself, but I love it."

Skylar hadn't known Amanda long, but the haircut and color, the new clothes, shoes, and jewelry had definitely lifted her spirits. And the way she grinned while her dance partner spun and whirled her on the parquet floor—well, she looked radiant.

Jinx watched his mom with a foul expression. "What's up with that guy?" He turned back to Skylar.

"What do you mean? They're having fun."

"Why's he so into her?"

"Um, because she's beautiful and they have a lot in common." He was being protective, and it was adorable. "They're a good match."

The moment Amanda had entered the club, with its black banquettes and gaudy chandeliers, the walls covered with signed photos of the rat pack, she'd lit up. A fifties-style band played "Come Fly with Me," and she danced with the owner of the car racing facility. He was the one who'd told Skylar about this place, had thought Amanda might like it.

He was right.

"If he thinks my mom's just some hookup—"

She rested her hand on his arm. "No, he doesn't. He's fifty-nine-years-old. His wife of thirty years died five years ago, and it took him a long time to even think about dating. The past year he's been going out because his kids are worried about him."

"You got all this while I went to the bathroom?"

She smiled. "No, it took longer than that. But you were too busy watching your mom smoke all the other drivers on the track." She tipped her chin to the dance floor. "Look at her."

Gavin swirled Amanda around the dance floor. He dipped her, and her leg kicked out. She laughed as she settled back in his arms, her new haircut letting her hair swing right back into place.

Jinx watched in disbelief. "I've never seen her like this."

"I think she's going to be okay. Even if she never sees Gavin again, she's had this night—this whole day—to open her eyes to a world of possibilities."

"She thanked me." He seemed a little choked up. He reached for his gin and tonic but didn't drink. "She said when she first moved here, she went out to dinner a couple times and saw a few of the sights, but nothing really interested her. The clubs with loud music and flashy clothes, the restaurants, the casinos…it wasn't her scene. But today, you opened up a whole new world for her." He reached for her hand. "She's going to call that company about being a test driver." Emotion gripped his features. "I've wanted her out of the ER for years. On one level, she's trying to keep people who've been in terrible accidents alive, since she couldn't be there for her husband and son. But, on another, she's reliving it every single day. I've wanted her to move on, to see a whole new canvas, for so damn long."

She couldn't help it. She brushed the hair off his forehead. "Kind of like Lori did for you?"

"No." He grabbed her wrist. "*You* did that. I would never have gone out with Lori if you hadn't knocked me on my ass so hard." He kissed her hand, the look in his eyes saying, *It's you. It's always been you.*

"I'm so glad I could help you date other women." *Oh,*

shit. She'd meant it as a joke, but when his eyebrows shot up, she heard how bitter she'd sounded. And, in that moment, she knew it was time to let the past go. If she wanted anything to develop between her and Jinx, she had to let go of the hurt and fear. "I was so jealous when I saw you and Lori together. I knew I had no right to be. I just…I'd gotten used to you wanting me, I hadn't expected it to go away and…when it did, it hurt."

"It never went away. Never will." He cupped her chin. "This afternoon, when my mom was in the dressing room, you said 'it's big this thing, us.' You were going to say something else. What was it?"

This is my chance. Take it. "That what we have…it's so much more than simple attraction. And that's what scares me. I…" She reached for a sugar packet and tapped it on the white tablecloth. "Ugh. I'm going to sound like a mess."

"You're the least messy person I know."

"In most ways, you're right. But in this one—relationships? I'm a big, complicated mess. The biggest problem for me is, if we don't work out…if we break up or you leave town…Rocco couldn't handle that."

The truth hit her like a wall of ocean water, knocking her back so hard she lost her breath. "Oh, my God." She tossed the sugar packet, shook her head. "It's not Rocco I'm protecting. It's me. I'm the one who couldn't handle falling for you the way I know I would—because this connection we have? It's just so strong. And if I open my heart again… you don't know. I love so hard, Jinx. So hard."

"I sure as fuck do know. You think I don't see how much you love your son? Your brother…your family? I want that, Sky. And you can bet, if you trust me with that kind of love,

I will never take it for granted. Not for a second. Because I'm going to treat you like a queen. I'm going to make sure you know every single minute of every day that you're the most beautiful person on this earth." He grabbed her other hand. "I'm crazy about you, Skylar James. The only time—" He closed his mouth, the muscle in his jawing flexing.

She moved closer to him. "The only time what?"

The intensity in his eyes burned right through to her heart, giving her a punch of adrenaline. "The only time I'm at peace is when I'm with you. Every day, I go through the motions. My life's separated into all these little pieces, work, home, my mom. But when I'm with you and Rocco, everything falls into place, and I feel whole."

"*Rocco*?" Did he even know what he just said?

"Yes, when I'm with the two of you…why are you looking at me like that?"

"You feel whole with *us*…not just with me?"

"Rocco is you. I want the whole package."

Dead. Skylar James was dead. This man…holy mother of God. Her lower lip trembled, and there was nothing she could do to keep the tears from spilling hot onto her cheeks. "You're…God, Jinx."

"Yeah. I feel the same way. Come on." He slid out of the booth. "Let's dance."

"You want to dance right now?"

He drew her into his arms, snugged her right up against him. He lowered his head and closed his eyes. "It's either that or make out with you at the table. You don't know how hard it is not to touch you."

"Oh, yes, I do."

He rested his forehead on hers. "Yeah? You want to

touch me? Because there's nothing stopping you. You can touch me all you want."

"I'm pretty sure we'd be kicked out if I touched you where I want."

He exhaled a hot, drawn-out *fuck* right at her ear. Wrapping his arms around her waist, his hands splayed on the top swells of her ass, he pressed his hips to hers. "You're killing me."

The feel of his hard cock against her stomach sent a sharp spike of arousal through her. She clung to him, forcing herself not to move her hips to get the friction she desperately needed.

"I like everything about you. The way you smell." He held her tighter, and she could feel the tremble in his arms. "Your hair. It's feisty, just like you. I like the way your eyes light up when you see my mom happy." He pressed her closer to him. "I want you, Skylar Bennington James."

She tipped her head back to see him better. "You know my middle name?"

"'Skylar Bennington James, you put that down right this minute.'"

She laughed at the way he mimicked her mom's tone whenever she was angry at her children. Dropping her forehead to his shoulder, she wrapped her arms around his neck. "I want you, too, Jackson Costello." A shiver tripped down her spine, creating a wave throughout her entire body. "I like you too much."

He tipped her chin. "How much?"

He'd opened his heart to her, and it was time she did the same. "I'm ready."

He looked confused. "For?"

"I'm done fighting my feelings for you. It was easy to push you away when it was nothing more than physical attraction. You're gorgeous, and you've got a body to die for. Those things I could resist. But you're the kindest, sweetest, most generous man I've ever known. And…" Tears burned.

"No, no more tears. I can't take it."

She shook her head. She needed to say this. "But you're so good with my son." She held his gaze, and emotion swelled so big and hard she couldn't contain it. "I like you so much, Jinx, and I…" She got up on her toes, clasped a hand around his neck and drew his mouth down to hers. "I really want to kiss you."

The first brush of lips sent sparks shooting through her. This big, hard muscled man was so gentle, his lips soft. He kissed her like she was a precious thing, like he wanted to savor this moment he'd waited so long for.

But she was too needy, too desperate for him. Licking the seam of his mouth, she felt a shudder run through his body. When their tongues collided, the world burst into a shower of stars, and—*Oh, my God*—she'd never wanted anyone the way she wanted him. "You think your mom will mind if we leave without her?"

Grabbing her hand, he led her across the dance floor and whispered into his mom's ear. She glanced to Skylar, looking concerned.

When he came back to her, she said, "What did you tell your mom?"

"I might've said I needed to get you to bed."

"You what?" She nudged him. "You did *not* tell your mom we're leaving to have sex."

He grinned. "She thinks you're not feeling well."

"Thank God."

Right there on the dance floor, he cupped her chin, forcing her to look him in the eyes. "Just so we're clear, I get that you're away from your son, you're in Vegas, and you want to have some fun. But I don't want an hour with you. I don't want one night."

"What do you want?"

"Everything." His desire for her made her knees buckle. "I want everything with you."

6

Jinx kicked the door shut, bent his knees, and lifted Skylar into his arms. Pressing her against the wall, he kissed her with relief and hunger, along with a roiling panic that wouldn't subside.

After tonight, he couldn't go back to a life without her. If she only wanted one night, if she got spooked by her trust issues again, it would destroy him.

Her fingers gripped the hair at the back of his neck, and she ground herself against him, her desperate moans winding him up and drowning his concerns. For now, at least, she was in this with him.

After two years of rejection, to finally be with her…it made it that much hotter.

"Come here." Gently, he set her down and led her to the bed. Throwing the covers back, he sat down to untie his boots and kick them off. He pulled his long-sleeve T-shirt over his head and reached for the top button of his jeans. When he noticed her standing there, watching, his hands stilled. Fear sliced through him. "What?" Was she changing her mind?

"Sometimes, in the summer, you take your shirt off in the garage, and I just about die. You are *so* hot. I could look at you all night."

"Yeah?" He got up, popping open the buttons and jerking the jeans off his hips.

Her eyes went wide. "Commando?" She fixed her gaze on his hard cock. "Oh, my God, Jinx. Look at you. I don't even know where to begin."

That greedy little smile. *Fuck me.* Skylar James was the sexiest woman he'd ever seen. Not just her physical beauty, but her mischievous smile, her compassion, her generosity. Everything about her turned him on. "We've got all the time in the world."

Lifting the dress over her head, she tossed it onto the floor. Her breasts jiggled inside the cups of her bra, and his hands ached to feel their heavy weight. She reached behind her for the clasp, and blood surged into his cock making him harder than he'd ever been in his life.

His body a live wire of need, he couldn't wait another second. Lunging for her, he grabbed her wrist and tumbled her onto the mattress. He smothered her cry of surprise with a kiss that sent a lightning strike through his body.

His senses heightened, he found himself awash in her floral scent, the silkiness of her hair, and smoothness of her skin. "I can't believe I get to kiss you."

She clutched him. "I'm scared."

He brushed the hair off her forehead. "Of what? I won't do anything you're not ready for."

"Of how much I feel...of you moving on...hurting

Rocco." She let out a breath. "Hurting me. I don't think I could stand it if you left."

"That's not going to happen. I only moved around because I didn't have a reason to stay. But you and Rocco… you give me roots. I want us." He kissed her temple, ran his nose across her cheek, and kissed the corner of her mouth. "You gonna give me a chance?"

She grew restless beneath him. "Yes." Fingers sliding into his hair, she drew him down for another kiss. "God, yes."

He yanked her panties down, and she kicked them aside, leaving her naked. He took in her pale skin against the white sheets, the sexy curve of her waist and flare of her hips. "Tell me you're mine."

"I'm *all* yours."

He pushed her breasts together, sucking a nipple into his mouth. One hand slid between her legs, seeking her slick heat. When he stroked her wet crease, she gasped, her hips arching off the mattress. He shifted his mouth to the other nipple, all while caressing her.

Her hips rocked insistently, and he pressed a trail of kisses down her stomach. Spreading her knees wider, he licked inside her.

"Oh, my God, Jinx." She gripped his hair.

Finding her hard nub, he licked fast, then slow, learning her body, her responses, and he didn't think he'd ever been happier. He reached for her breasts, flicked his thumbs over her nipples, and kissed her the same way he'd just loved her mouth.

"I can't believe…I'm going to come already." Lust saturated her tone, making it almost sound dreamy. "Jinx…*oh, my God*." Her hips snapped up, and she pressed herself against his mouth, her hands holding his head in place. "Don't stop, don't stop, don't—" She cried out, hips swiveling. Her body seized, and then her ass dropped to the mattress. "Holy shit."

With her flushed cheeks and sleepy eyes, she looked sated and happy. He smoothed the hair off her cheek, traced her lips with a finger. "You're so fucking beautiful."

Cupping the back of his head, she drew him in for another kiss, and elation overwhelmed him. She reached for his cock, her warm grasp making his body clench with desire. "Hang on." He leaned off the side of the bed, snagging his jeans and pulling out his wallet.

"Let me do it." She sat up, those sexy breasts bouncing, and he loved her like this, so uninhibited, so free. She dangled the foil packet in front of him. "All right, you have two choices. This…" She tore it open with her teeth and pulled out the condom. "Or my mouth? Which do you want covering this bad boy?" She stroked him, letting her thumb glide around the head of his cock. "Choose wisely."

Is this happening? Lust surged, and he rolled onto his back. "Suck me."

Grasping his cock, she licked it from the root to the head, before taking him into the slick heat of her mouth. She watched him, eyes shining with desire and mischief. Her tongue flicked and swirled, and his hips shot off the mattress. "Fuck, Skylar."

Those big brown eyes turned sultry as her hands tugged him in rhythm with the hungry pulls of her tongue. He'd never been more aroused in his life. His body vibrated with lust and love and want and need.

This is Skylar.

Fucking my cock with her mouth.

And loving it.

He got that stab of fear again.

She faltered, pulling him out, her lips shiny and swollen. "What's wrong?"

"Nothing." He reached for the back of her head. "Go on."

"No. Not until you talk to me." She sat up. "If we're going to work, we have to be honest with each other. I need that. You have no idea how much."

"*Are* we going to work? When we get home, are we going to be together—or is this a Vegas thing?"

She straddled his lap, scraping the hair back from his temples. "We're together. I want this. I want us. I love how you are with Rocco. I love the way you look at me. I love the way you never gave up on me. Mostly, I just love the man you are. You're so strong and steady and smart and creative and…God, you're the best man I've ever known."

He lurched forward. "I'm going to love you so hard, and I'm going to be the best fucking dad Rocco could ever want."

"That's the thing. I know that. I *know* it." She rolled the condom on with shaky hands. As she sank down on him, she let out a hiss of breath. "*Yes.*" And then she was moving, a slow, steady rhythm, her head tilting back in pleasure.

Mesmerized by how beautiful she looked lost in pleasure, he wanted to watch her forever, but he couldn't take it anymore. He needed friction. He needed to come. "I'm gonna fuck you right now, okay?"

"Yes. Please."

No more talking, he grabbed her ass, lifted her, and

slammed her down on him. Sensation exploded, driving him for more, faster. He fucked her so hard her tits bounced, and she reached for the headboard, slamming down on him, meeting his wild thrusts.

This woman…she was the one for him. No question. He'd give her all the time she needed, but one day, they'd get married. And, if she wanted it, they'd have a baby together.

And he'd have her forever.

He toppled her onto her back, lifted her leg over his hip, and drove into her. His balls tightened, and his spine tingled, and he knew he wasn't going to last. Reaching between them, he found her clit and stroked her into a climax that had her back arching, her body writhing.

Skylar lost in desire was the most beautiful thing he'd ever seen. And then he slammed home, as he came so hard his vision splintered into dazzling white stars.

He collapsed beside her, wrapping an arm around her waist and pulling her close. Tucking his face into her neck, he sighed.

He'd waited so long…had almost given up believing he could ever have this kind of happiness. And here he was.

I got the girl.

And I'm never letting go.

EPILOGUE

It never failed. Every night, as she turned onto her street, Skylar peered into the front bay window of her pretty little house with the flower beds and glider on the porch.

For so many years, she'd get glimpses of family life from other people's windows. A mom rocking a baby, a cocktail party, a family sitting down for dinner. Her heart would squeeze because she never believed she'd get to have that life. Worse, that Rocco would grow up without a dad or siblings.

She glanced at the white plastic CVS bag on the passenger seat. Emotion flooded her so hard she had to blink back the sting of tears. *I have it all.*

I can't believe it.

She never dreamed she could have so much joy.

Hitting the button to open the garage, she drove in, parking right alongside Jinx's badass black SUV. She cut the engine, grabbed her purse and the pharmacy bag, and then headed into her home, expecting the usual ruckus of Jinx and Rocco building a pillow fort or chasing each other with Nerf guns.

Tonight, though, it was quiet. Other than the gentle hum of the refrigerator, she didn't hear a single sound. Which was odd. And it fired up her nerves.

She glanced at the dinner dishes, disturbed to find Rocco's uneaten.

What's going on? Dropping her purse and the bag, she opened her mouth to shout for them, when she heard a deep voice murmuring. Hurrying down the hallway, she saw the spill of yellow light on the hardwood floor outside Rocco's room.

"I'll be honest with you," Jinx said quietly, gently. "It hurts my heart to see you sad."

"I'm not sad." Rocco sounded grumpy, impatient.

"You should know, if something's happening at school, and you don't want to tell me about it because you're worried I'll get involved or embarrass you, you could tell me that. You can always come to me and your mom and say, Hey, man, I need to talk to you, but I want you to promise not to tell anyone. You can always say that to us."

"School's fine."

"Well, okay. I hear your words, but they don't match your expression, so that's why I'm worried. You need some time alone, I'll give it to you. I just want you to know that you can tell me anything."

Skylar wanted to barge in and press Rocco for an answer, but she'd follow Jinx's lead on this one. He was so much more patient. Her instinct was always to burn down the world for her son, where Jinx wanted to teach Rocco how to navigate it.

Jinx. God, he was a good man. The best. Sometimes she couldn't believe he was hers.

And that she'd almost pushed him away.

Her heart clutched at the thought. If he hadn't asked her to go to Vegas…

But he had. And she'd gone.

And now…nearly a year later, they were together. And it was so damn good.

"I'm going to wash the dishes," Jinx said. "I'll leave your plate for last, in case you get hungry." His shadow fell onto the hallway, as he neared the door. "I love you, Rocco."

She froze, holding her breath so they wouldn't hear her eavesdropping.

But he didn't leave the room.

Because her son said, "Jinx?"

"Yes?"

Rocco didn't say anything, and the silence was excruciating. What was troubling her little boy? He'd been quieter than usual the past couple of days. But he wouldn't say what was on his mind.

And Jinx…God, he just gave her little boy all the space in the world, while letting him know he was safe and loved.

I love him. With everything I am, I love Jinx Costello.

And I want his name. I want all three of us to have the same name.

"Jinx?" Rocco said again.

"Yes." To hear that big, strong, tattooed man use such a gentle voice with her shy boy never failed to turn her into a puddle of love.

"Will you come here?"

"You bet."

Skylar couldn't take it anymore. She inched closer to the doorway and peered in.

Jinx crossed the room and sat on the edge of the mattress. His big hand cupped Rocco's cheek, and her son gazed up at him with a tortured expression.

Had he done something wrong? God, he was only five years old. What trouble could he have gotten into? His preschool teacher hadn't said anything.

Finally, her boy said, "Are you…going to live here forever?"

The breath whooshed out of Skylar's lungs, and she squeezed her hands into fists. They'd talked about Jinx moving in, about him being part of their little family, but it hadn't occurred to her that Rocco didn't know it was permanent.

"I am. I'm going to be here forever. You know why? Because I love your mom, and I love you. Nothing makes me happier than being with you two."

But she didn't see relief on Rocco's features. And Jinx obviously didn't either because he withdrew his hand. "Do you not want me here forever? You can tell me the truth. I won't be angry."

"I want…" Her son swallowed, his little hands squeezing the blue and white striped comforter.

Jinx tipped his chin up. "You can tell me anything. Whatever you have to say, I'm going to be okay with it. I don't have to live here. If you want me to move to an apartment, if you want it to just be you and your mom again, I can do that. I'd still like to be in your lives. I'd like to have dinner with you—"

"No, I don't…that's not what I mean." Rocco's cheeks

burned red. "I want you…"

Dammit, Rocco's voice turned to a whisper, and she missed the last several words.

"Yeah?" Jinx's voice cracked.

Rocco nodded energetically.

"Rocco, man, I want that more than anything in the world." Jinx scooped him into his arms, and they clung to each other.

With his cheek pressed to Jinx's shoulder, he said, "Can I call you Daddy?"

"Yeah, son." Jinx's voice cracked. "Nothing would make me happier."

He patted Jinx's broad back. "Okay, Daddy."

Hot tears spilled down her cheeks. She thought she'd been happy before. But this…

This was it.

Her world was complete.

She thought of the CVS bag and smiled. Maybe she'd hold off for a few weeks before she told them.

Give them a little time to bond as father and son…

Before adding another baby to the family.

Thank you for reading COME AWAY WITH ME! If you want a glimpse of Jinx's first year in Calamity, when he was crushing on Skylar, and she pretended to want nothing to do with him, check out JUST THE WAY YOU ARE, the story of a princess gone wild—and the badass athlete who falls madly in love with her.

Up next is WHOLE LOTTA LOVE, where a quiet,

introverted chef finally lives her life out loud with a hot, sexy quarterback.

Need more Calamity Falls, the western capital of whoop-ass, where the people are wild at heart?

KEEP ON LOVING YOU
WE BELONG TOGETHER
THE VERY THOUGHT OF YOU
JUST THE WAY YOU ARE
IT WAS ALWAYS YOU
CAN'T HELP FALING IN LOVE
COME AWAY WITH ME
WHOLE LOTTA LOVE

Have you read the Rock Star Romance series? Come meet the sexy rockers of Blue Fire:

YOU REALLY GOT ME
I WANT YOU TO WANT ME
TAKE ME HOME TONIGHT
MORE THAN A FEELING

And Erika Kelly's super passionate Wild Love series:

MINE FOR NOW
MINE FOR THE WEEK
MINE FOREVER

Look for WHOLE LOTTA LOVE in January 2021! Sign up for my newsletter to get a FREE copy of PLANES, TRAINS, AND HEAD OVER HEELS. And come hang out with me on Facebook, Twitter, Instagram, Goodreads, and Pinterest or in my private reader group.

WHOLE LOTTA LOVE

PROLOGUE

Winter Sophomore Year

Her fiancé burst into laughter, and Lulu Cavanaugh turned to watch him across the crowded restaurant. Surrounded by her dad and his football buddies, he was totally in his element.

Happiness spread through her in a dizzying rush, and she had to cover her mouth to hide a huge, dopey smile. That tall, gorgeous, life-of-the-party man had chosen *her* to spend his life with. And she didn't know how she'd gotten so lucky.

I'll never be alone again.

The thought came out of nowhere, delivering a stark relief that nearly buckled her knees. She thought about all those New Year's Eves when her sisters—gorgeous and glittering—would race out the door with their boyfriends, leaving her home alone. The countless Valentine's Days when her roommates would dress up for romantic evenings, leaving her alone in a cloud of perfume.

She'd never feel that painful loneliness again.

Because tomorrow she'd marry Trace Heller.

Look at him.

How in the world did I get a guy like that? Starting linebacker for Penn State, big man on campus, he was genuinely nice, smart, and funny. Everybody liked him—professors, students…the cafeteria staff had a smoothie ready for him every morning at six AM—and it wasn't even on the menu. He was the golden boy.

And he's mine.

An arm wrapped around her shoulder and tugged her in close. "I don't think I've ever seen you so happy."

Lulu tucked her face into the crook of her older sister's neck. *I am happy.* She clasped Gigi's wrist. "Thank you for being here."

Gigi released her. "What kind of thing is that to say? Of course I'm here." The lead singer for an all-girl pop band, her oldest sister was in the middle of a world tour. She had virtually no control over her life—down to how she dressed and the color of her hair—so it really was a big deal. "You excited for tomorrow? Actually, knowing you, you're probably more excited about the honeymoon."

Joy bubbled through her at the thought of Tokyo, where she got to spend time in the kitchens of Michelin-starred chefs. Yet another reason to love her future husband—he didn't mind her cooking on three of their vacation nights.

"I just want to get the production over with." Lulu preferred a small, intimate wedding, but Trace and his family had fought her hard on that—they had hundreds of people they absolutely could not "snub."

Her fiancé came by his outgoing nature honestly—his parents and siblings were all big-time extroverts. They lived on a cul-de-sac in Iowa that threw weekly block parties all summer long, and their house was party central during football season.

She'd conceded, of course. Lots of people found her quiet intensity a turn-off, so if he accepted her, she could absolutely respect his big personality—even when it meant she didn't have his full attention when they went out together.

When it meant she had to walk down the aisle with three hundred and fifty people watching her.

Trace lifted his arms, executing a sexy swivel of his hips, as if dancing to a Snoop Dog song. *He's the brightest light in any room.* His welcoming grin served as an invitation. *Come party with me. We'll have a blast.*

A red dress in her peripheral vision grabbed her attention, and she spotted her younger sister in a heated conversation.

As Stella drained a champagne flute, her boyfriend's big hand closed around her wrist and tried to pull the glass away from her mouth. Nobody tamed the gorgeous, wild eighteen-year old, though, so she twirled out of his reach. Stella wobbled on those ridiculously high heels, but Griffin grabbed her, wrapped an arm around her waist and hauled her up hard against him. He lowered his mouth to her ear, and her expression turned sultry, wicked, before she elbowed him in the stomach and freed herself. Just as he started to walk away in anger, Stella fisted his dress shirt and jerked him back, cupping his neck and kissing him like they were alone in her bedroom.

God, they were a fiery, passionate couple.

"She's drunk," Gigi said.

"I know, and it's so weird." Normally, Stella would be right by her side. Her best friend and fiercest protector, her sister made sure to stay close in social situations so Lulu didn't wind up standing alone in a corner. Nobody got her like Stella did. "Why would she do this at my rehearsal dinner?"

"Oh, come on. She's afraid of losing you."

That's ridiculous. Lulu had always needed Stella—not the other way around. "She knows better than that." Unlike her sister, Lulu didn't have a million acquaintances. She had Trace, her family, and a few close friends. And she was fiercely loyal to them all. "But she's going to feel like crap tomorrow." *When I'll need her with me.*

She's my maid of honor.

"Let me go talk to her." But before Gigi could go, Stella caught them staring and broke away from her boyfriend.

Her hair a sexy tousle of chestnut waves, she rushed up to them. "The tank is full, and my car's right out front. Say the word…" With that devilish glint in her eyes—anyone would take Stella's comment as light and jovial.

But not Lulu. She knew Stella down to her very soul, and her sister wasn't joking. She'd been against Trace from the very first time Lulu had brought him home. "Nope. Not going anywhere." And then she looked her sister right in the eyes, so she'd finally hear her. "I love him, Stella. I *want* to marry him."

Any pretense of joking flatlined, and Stella's expression grew desperate. Grabbing Lulu's arm, she forced her to face her fiancé. "Look at him. Why's he hanging around dad's friends and not you? It's your rehearsal dinner. Shouldn't he be by your side?"

"We don't have that kind of relationship." *Which is why it works.*

"What does that even mean? You're going to spend your life with this man."

"That's right. And we work *because* we're so different. What guy would put up with spending three nights of our honeymoon apart from me? Trace loves my passion for food, and he likes that we're not joined at the hip. It means he can go out and party and do his thing without having to take care of a clingy girlfriend. Do you know how freeing it is to do what I love without worrying that I'm leaving him alone too much? Stella, he sees me. And he likes what he sees." It felt good to say it out loud. It empowered her.

Trace is the right man for me.

He chose *me.*

Stella leaned forward, reeking of wine. "If he likes you so much, then why does he flirt with *me*?"

God.

No one can hurt you worse than the people who know you best.

Lulu fought back the rising swell of humiliation and fear. She pressed her trembling hands to her stomach. *Don't let her ruin this night for you.* "He flirts with everyone. That's just who he is."

"You're drunk, Stella," Gigi said. "Not a good look for the maid of honor."

"Why are you defending him, when you know I'm right?" Stella grew frantic. "You're all out of your mind to let her go through with this wedding." She grabbed Lulu's hands. "I want you to be happy—you know I do—I *love* you—but this guy is not who you think he is."

"Stop it." Gigi's voice was low, threatening.

"No, I'm not going to stop." Stella grabbed her hands and squeezed. "This is *me*. You have to know I would never hurt you. I'm trying to *save* you. He's not who you want him to be. He's just not."

Lulu was shaking, but it wasn't from fear. "I know exactly who he is. He *flirts,* but he doesn't act on it. And you, of all people, should know that because he's just like you. He's the life of the party, but he's also loyal and just as protective of me as you are."

"God, Lulu." Stella practically shouted. "You're only seeing what you want—"

"No." Wrenching her hands free, Lulu took a step back. "Your job as maid of honor—as my *sister*—isn't to tell me what's right or wrong for me. Your job is to stand beside me, and if things go sideways, you can hand me a pint of cookies and cream ice cream, two spoons, and a box of Kleenex. But I'm telling you right now, if you can't support me, then you won't be at my side at the altar tomorrow."

Lulu turned away from them, making a beeline for the kitchen.

"What is your problem?" she heard Gigi say.

"How can you stand here and let her make the biggest mistake of her life?" Stella said. "Why is everyone acting like this wedding is okay?"

The back of her neck prickled, as though the eyes of everyone in the restaurant were on her, pitying her. As if they all knew something she didn't about Trace.

But it wasn't true. She did know him.

He'd grown up in a family obsessed with football—of course he was starstruck around her dad and his friends. What was wrong with that? She *wanted* him to be close to her family.

And he flirted with everybody—the bus driver for away games, the security guard at the mall. *That's just who he is.*

Unused to high heels and tight dresses, she grew self-conscious and wished like hell she'd been born with a tenth of Stella's confidence and style.

But she hadn't been, so she sought the comfort of the one place on earth she felt like her best self. Pushing through the doors, the heat hit her first, followed by the scents of grilled meat and chopped herbs. Nothing soothed her like being in the beating heart of a restaurant, with the steam rising, oil sizzling, and everyone busy at their stations.

Here, she felt competent and in control. She felt beautiful in the only way that mattered to her—she created dishes that made people sigh with delight.

Jonny Lee James, the owner and chef de cuisine, spotted

her. A big grin cracked his rugged features. Wiping his hands on a dish towel, he opened his arms and came towards her. "My sweet girl."

She fell against him, breathing in the scents of caramelized onions and sautéed garlic embedded in his chef's jacket.

"You come to boss me around?" Tipping his head, he grinned. "Make my béchamel sublime?"

But she didn't feel like joking, so she nestled in against him, comforted by those big, strong hands on her back. He got the message and held her instead of talking.

She should be happy. She should be on top of the world.

But she didn't think she could do that without Stella's support. Because, until Trace, her sister had always been the one Lulu relied on. In fifth grade, when Lulu had a crush on Danny Keene, Stella had invited him over for a playdate. Stella had been *eight years old*.

When Lulu didn't have a date for the junior prom, Stella had surprised her with a weekend in Seattle. They'd had an absolute blast, posting pictures on social media, so everyone would think she couldn't make the dance because of a trip with her mom and sister—not because no one had asked her.

So, for Stella to not like Trace—to not *trust* him—it meant something. She didn't want to choose between her husband and her sister. She shouldn't have to. But if Stella couldn't accept this marriage, this relationship…how would that work? Every time her sister and Trace were in the same room, would Stella accuse Trace of hitting on her? Would she start avoiding them?

Lulu needed her sister. Couldn't bear the thought of them growing apart.

"There she is." Her mom's voice rose above the kitchen noises. "I knew I'd find you here."

Chef Jonny pulled away to greet the tall, slender, and beautiful Joss Montalbano, a former Eighties supermodel who'd passed her poise and confidence on to all of her daughters, except one. *Me.*

"One day, she's going to get this place a Michelin star." Her mom beamed at her with so much pride, Lulu almost felt guilty for choosing Penn State over Le Cordon Bleu, as everyone had expected.

She probably should've gone to Paris, but she'd wanted so badly to be normal. To have fun and party and go wild. Unfortunately, it hadn't even taken one semester to accept that she just wasn't that person.

But she'd found Trace, and that had made attending a big university worthwhile.

"Trust me, she'll do much bigger and better things than The Homesteader Inn." Chef Jonny squeezed her shoulder.

Lulu shook her head. "If Michelin covered Wyoming, you'd have a star. No question." People came from all around the world to stay at the romantic inn nestled in the woods of the Teton Mountain Range. A twelve-course meal prepared by Chef Jonny was a treat—they were booked a year in advance.

"Well, come on, sweetie, we're about to do toasts," her mom said.

"Excellent." Chef Jonny untied his apron. "Let me find my wife, so she can open the champagne."

As her mom hooked an arm through hers and led her

out of the kitchen, Lulu glanced back over her shoulder and found Chef watching her with a concerned expression. That same awful longing welled up again, to stay in the kitchen, in the only world where she felt like her best self.

But that'll change tomorrow, when I get married. And then I'll never feel this loneliness again. No matter where I am, no matter what I'm doing, I'll know there's someone at home waiting for me.

They made their way to the head table, where her dad talked with his buddies.

Her mom leaned in. "Where's Trace?"

"No idea." She'd ask her dad. "Do you know where Trace went?"

He spun around with a big smile. Everyone loved Tyler Cavanaugh, not because he was one of the best quarterbacks who'd ever played, but because he listened to their stories. He cared. He was such a good guy. "Uh…he was here a minute ago." Reaching for Lulu, he enfolded her in his big, strong arms. "Before we do toasts, I just want to say something. Tomorrow, I'm symbolically giving you away, but you'll always be my little girl. You know that, right?"

She nodded against his chest. When he was about to pull away, she looked up at him. "Do you think I'm making a mistake marrying Trace?"

He grew instantly alert, as though hearing a burglar in the house. "We've talked about this before." He searched her eyes. "You know my concerns, but you said you loved him and wanted to be with him. Why are you bringing it up now, the night before the wedding?" His sincere expression drew a sting of tears to the backs of her eyes. "If you're having second thoughts, tell me now. I don't care how far along it's gotten, we'll call it off, no problem."

"No, no. I'm not calling anything off. I just want to know…never mind." He was right. Multiple times over the past eighteen months, he'd suggested Trace was spending way too much time with him, and Lulu had told him she liked that he fit in so well, that it gave her the freedom to cook and the comfort to know they'd always live close to her family—not his.

"You sure?" Her dad looked concerned.

"Positive."

He gave her a nod, trusting her, and then reached for a knife, tapping it against his water glass. "Can everyone take a seat, please? Champagne's coming around, so grab a glass."

Chairs scraped, and the conversation grew even louder as people looked for their tables.

"Has anyone seen Trace?" her mom asked.

One of her dad's football buddies, cupped his mouth and called, "Trace? Where's the groom?"

A server with a pewter tray brought glasses filled with bubbly to the head table, and Lulu grabbed hers. Excitement started to roll in, as she pushed aside her doubts and focused on the moment.

"Oh, good," she heard her mom say. "You're here."

She turned, eager to have Trace close, needing his reassurance. He always knew how to make her feel special.

But it wasn't him. It was Gigi. "You're giving the first toast," her mom said.

Nodding, Gigi reached for a glass. She took a sip, eyeing Lulu over the top of the flute with a saucy shrug of her platinum eyebrows.

I should've chosen Gigi as my maid of honor.

"Should I text him?" Lulu asked.

Gigi shook her head. "Why bother? He's not paying attention to his phone right now. Not with all his buddies here to party with him."

Searching the room, her dad cupped his hands at either side of his mouth and called, "Trace!"

But between the shadows created by the low lighting, the potted plants, and the wait staff setting bread baskets on the tables, it was hard to make out individual faces.

Any minute now, he'd pop his head out from a big group of people—probably at the bar—and he'd jog across the restaurant, bumping fists and slapping palms on his way to the head table.

"I'm starting without him." Her dad faced the room. "Can I get everyone to sit down?" His commanding presence had people quieting down. "Thank you all for coming tonight. It's great to see faces we haven't seen in a while." He shoved a hand into the pocket of his dress slacks. "Lulu came out of the womb with a spatula in one hand and a sprig of parsley in the other." He paused for the titter of laughter. "And her first word was, 'kitchen,' breaking her mother's heart."

Laughter erupted, and her dad continued talking. But noise filled her brain. There were only a few people still standing, and Trace wasn't with them.

"Right, sweetheart?" Her dad wrapped an arm around her shoulder and drew her up against him. She'd missed that last sentence, but the guests were laughing, so she didn't have to answer. She just stood there and smiled.

And that's when her gaze snagged on a red dress.

She did a double-take.

Because at the back of the restaurant, behind the fronds of a potted plant, right where the tiny, white fairy lights dripped down the stucco walls, Stella was making out with someone that wasn't Griffin.

Lulu went rigid. She had to take a moment to make sense of what she was seeing because her mind was tricking her into seeing Trace.

Lots of men wore crisp blue suits. Lots of them had neatly trimmed blonde hair.

But none of them wore a neon yellow silicone wristband signifying the Penn State football team's annual fundraiser for The Children's House.

"Now," her dad said. "I'm going to hand the mic over to Gigi, who's got a little story to tell."

But time had stopped. A clammy chill gripped her skin.

"Lu?" Her dad squeezed her shoulder. "What's going on?"

Clothing swished and chairs screeched on the hardwood floor, as everyone followed Lulu's gaze to the back of the room. Trace's hands clutched Stella's ass, squeezing, as he ground his hips against her.

"That fucker." Coco charged across the room. "I'm going to cut his dick off."

"Is that Trace?" her mom asked. "Who is he…is that *Stella*?"

"Oh, my God," someone called.

In the flurry of activity—her sister racing across the room, people jumping out of their seats—Lulu set her flute down on the table. A commotion broke out when one of Trace's friends pulled him off Stella.

Quietly, Lulu headed around the table. Eyes on the bright red exit sign, her legs moved, and it was all she could do to stay upright, as the weight of a hundred suns bore down on her.

Two years ago, Stella had stolen Griffin right out from her.

Tonight, her sister had stolen her future.

And this time, there was no going back.

ABOUT THE AUTHOR

Award-winning author Erika Kelly writes sexy and emotional small town romance. Married to the love of her life and raising four children, she lives in the southwest, drinks a lot of tea, and is always waiting for her cats to get off her keyboard.

https://www.erikakellybooks.com/

facebook.com/erikakellybooks

twitter.com/ErikaKellyBooks

instagram.com/erikakellyauthor

goodreads.com/Erika_Kelly

pinterest.com/erikakellybooks

amazon.com/Erika-Kelly

bookbub.com/authors/erika-kelly

Made in the USA
Monee, IL
14 September 2020

41253173R00080